Praise for
KRISTINE KATHRYN RUSCH'S DIVING UNIVERSE

"The Diving Universe, conceived by Hugo-Award winning author Kristine [Kathryn] Rusch is a refreshingly new and fleshed out realm of sci-fi action and adventure."

—Astroguyz

"Kristine Kathryn Rusch is best known for her Retrieval Artist series, so maybe you've missed her Diving Universe series. If so, it's high time to remedy that oversight."

—Analog

"This is classic sci-fi, a well-told tale of dangerous exploration. The first-person narration makes the reader an eye witness to the vast, silent realms of deep space, where even the smallest error will bring disaster. Compellingly human and technically absorbing, the suspense builds to fevered intensity, culminating in an explosive yet plausible conclusion."

—RT Book Reviews (Top Pick) on *Diving into the Wreck*

"Rusch delivers a page-turning space adventure while contemplating the ethics of scientists and governments working together on future tech."

—Publishers Weekly on *Diving into the Wreck*

"Rusch's handling of the mystery and adventure is stellar, and the whole tale proves quite entertaining."

—Booklist Online on *Diving into the Wreck*

"The technicalities in Boss' story are beautifully played.... She's real, flawed, and interesting.... Read the book. It is very good."

—SFFWorld on *Diving into the Wreck*

"Kristine Kathryn Rusch's *Diving into the Wreck* is exactly what the sf genre needs to get more readers…and to keep the readers the genre already has."
—*Elitist Book Reviews* on *Diving into the Wreck*

"Rusch keeps the science accessible, the cultures intriguing, and the characters engaging. For anyone needing to add to their science fiction library, keep an eye out for this."
—*Speculative Fiction Examiner* on *City of Ruins*

"Rusch's latest addition to her Diving series features a strong, capable female heroine and a vividly imagined far-future universe. Blending fast-paced action with an exploration of the nature of friendship and the ethics of scientific discoveries, this tale should appeal to Rusch's readers and fans of space opera."
—*Library Journal* on *Boneyards*

"Rusch follows *Diving into the Wreck* and *City of Ruins* with another fast-paced novel of the far future… [Rusch's] sensibilities will endear this book to readers looking for a light, quick space adventure with strong female protagonists."
—*Publishers Weekly* on *Boneyards*

"Filled with well-defined characters who confront a variety of ethical and moral dilemmas, Rusch's third Diving novel is classic space opera, with richly detailed worldbuilding and lots of drama."
—*RT Book Reviews* on *Boneyards*

"…a fabulous outer space thriller that rotates perspective between the divers, the Alliance and to a lesser degree the Empire. Action-packed and filled with twists yet allowing the reader to understand the motives of the key players, *Skirmishes* is another intelligent exciting voyage into the Rusch Diving universe."
—*The Midwest Book Review* on *Skirmishes*

The Diving Universe

(Reading Order)

SQUISHY'S TEAMS

A DIVING UNIVERSE NOVEL

KRISTINE KATHRYN RUSCH

*wmg*PUBLISHING

Squishy's Teams

IMPORTANT AUTHOR'S NOTE

Before reading Squishy's Teams, *please read* Boneyards. *To understand part of* Squishy's Teams, *you will need to know the events of* Boneyards.

SQUISHY'S TEAMS

A DIVING UNIVERSE NOVEL

1

THREE MONTHS OF WORK.

Hallie Conifer stood in the middle of the ancient base, hands pressed against her aching back. The air still smelled stale here, no matter what she did to the environmental system. She'd spent the first week tweaking that, fixing the gravity so that she was comfortable, even though her colleague, István Gorka, found the gravity a bit too light.

The base, on the moon above Palmyra, hadn't been used in a very long time. It was old, even by Empire standards. The equipment was gray and heavy and counterintuitive. Every console had knobs and buttons, which was good on the one hand, because it meant that once she got power flowing through it all, nothing malfunctioned.

But she had to turn things and juggle things, and sometimes she had to pound on the old metal consoles just to get them to work. Room after room after room of consoles. It took her days to figure out which ones she actually needed.

Gorka had followed her through the rooms, a frown on his square face. He had large bones that made his brow hang heavy over his eyes. His cheeks were at right angles from his jaw, and his lips were thick, even when they were frowning at her in disapproval. His skin was pale when she met him, and now it was a bit gray, probably from the crap food they'd been eating.

Or maybe just from his attitude.

He hadn't liked anything she'd done, from getting the lighting system up and running to fixing the environmental system so that she could comfortably work here.

He hadn't realized that she was making the weapons system operational again. Or rather, that she was putting it back online. The weapons were the only part of this ancient base that had been operational from the moment she and Gorka had landed here.

Their initial trip to this moon had been a short stop before they headed down to Ubieks, the city on the edge of Desierto Amarillo. The desert covered most of a continent on Palmyra, a planet Conifer hadn't visited before.

She hadn't liked it—or rather, she hadn't liked Ubieks, even though she and Gorka had lived there for nearly a month, establishing themselves, finding a way to get to the research station housed deep inside the desert.

When they had finally gotten the chance to apply for jobs at the station, Gorka had blown his opportunity almost immediately. He had gone in, all cocky and strong, as if he knew better, and he had talked to the scientists—not as a potential employee, but as an equal.

And that had gotten him kicked out day one. When she had tried to apply as an intern, like Squishy had recommended, Conifer had been turned away as well. The desert station didn't want strangers on the site for any reason, and their experience with Gorka had made them more paranoid, not less.

So she and Gorka had retreated to the moon base. He had wanted to swap out with one of the other teams, but the orders were that no one was supposed to contact each other once they were in the field. After they had successfully completed their missions, they were to meet up at a designated point.

Until then, no contact allowed. Not that they could contact anyone. Squishy had made sure no one knew who was doing what.

Squishy had worked in the Enterran Empire for decades, and knew how their systems worked. She believed that anyone who got captured would get tortured, and would reveal what they knew.

2

So Squishy controlled the information. She was the only one who knew where all five backup sites were. She was the only one who knew where the main stealth tech research station was. She was the only one who knew the names of everyone involved, although they had all met, months ago.

That was when Squishy had paired them—one scientist/engineer and one security officer/muscle. Conifer was the scientist/engineer. Gorka was the muscle, as she kept reminding him.

The problem was that he believed he was her intellectual equal. And her moral superior.

He stood near the environmental controls for the weapons room, his back to the dirty gray walls. She had tried to keep him busy these last few months. She had assigned him to monitor the Desierto Amarillo Research Station—as it was called—to see the patterns of the employees there.

But most of the employees worked and lived onsite, which was making Gorka squeamish. She hadn't told him what she wanted to do, but he could guess.

Which was why he had his arms crossed right now, his narrow face filled with disapproval.

"I don't think they'll respond to an alarm triggered from here," he said, getting it wrong from the very start. The alarm that he wanted her to trigger wouldn't be triggered from this old base.

He had badgered her into digging into the systems of the Desierto Amarillo station—a risky maneuver that might have alerted the scientists below to her presence—and she had done that from the ship they had arrived in.

The equipment in this base was a century old, and the scientists below would have seen through anything she had done using the base's equipment.

She had to use the equipment that she and Gorka had brought because it was much more sophisticated than anything found in the Empire. She could mask what she did with her equipment, and no one on that station below would catch her.

Which was a good thing.

If the ship she and Gorka had brought had had the proper weaponry, she wouldn't need to use anything from this base at all. But the ship hadn't had that kind of weaponry—on purpose, as Gorka had reminded her.

Squishy hadn't wanted a large loss of life.

Squishy be damned.

Losing forty scientists on a research station no one cared about wouldn't matter at all, not compared to the lives saved by destroying what was *beneath* that station.

All of the backups of all of the Empire's stealth tech research. And if the other teams were as focused as Conifer was, and if they all succeeded—bigger ifs than she wanted to think about—then the lives saved would be in the tens of thousands, well worth the forty lives lost.

"Why don't you go trigger the alarm and see what they do?" Conifer said, mostly to get rid of him rather than to save any lives below. She had a few things to finish up before she launched the weapons.

It would be good to have him out of her way so she could concentrate.

"And if they don't leave, you'll call this off?" he asked.

"Sure," she lied.

He stared at her for a long moment, and she made the mistake of staring back. He clearly hated her as much as she hated him.

Three months alone in this place had exacerbated their differences rather than encouraging them to get along. They had stopped eating meals together in the ship after the first week, and he blamed her for that. He might have been right; she shouldn't have berated him for his ridiculously stupid lapse of judgement. It all was going to work out well. Once she used the weapons system from up here, the station would be obliterated, and that was so much better than the surgical strike Squishy had wanted them to carry out.

"You're not going to stop, are you?" he asked.

She didn't like his tone. He sounded almost like he was threatening her. Maybe he was.

He might be able to take her in a one-on-one battle, but it wouldn't come to that. She had already thought through the various scenarios, and she would stop him long before he got anywhere near her.

Besides, she'd seen him try to operate in this lower gravity. He couldn't quite find his center. His movements were never as assured as they had been before the two of them entered Empire space.

"Just set off your alarm," she said.

"You'll give them an hour to vacate the station?" he asked.

"I'll give them two," she said.

His eyes widened ever so slightly. Maybe she shouldn't have been so magnanimous. She hadn't been in the past, and he knew it.

She had to cover that mistake.

"I still have a lot of work to do before I can activate the weapons," she said.

He studied her for a long moment. She stared back at him.

Finally, he nodded, apparently believing her.

She had to work hard to prevent a smile. His lack of knowledge about systems, about the work she had already done, about *her*, was going to cost him.

And he didn't even realize it.

"Two hours," he said. "You promise?"

"Yes," she said. "I promise."

He hesitated one minute longer. Her impatience grew. She needed him out of here.

Then he pointed at her, as if reminding her yet again not to release the weapons until the station had a chance to evacuate.

She moved to the front of the weapons panel and slowly, ostentatiously, clasped her hands behind her back.

He glared at her one last time and left.

She waited until the door clanged shut before turning around and facing the controls on the weapons system. They were needlessly complicated, and it had taken her almost a week to set everything up, so that she could just hit the commands.

Then she heard something squeal behind her.

"I knew you were going to do that," Gorka said.

His voice came from closer to her than she expected. She turned, saw that he had a laser pistol, which surprised her.

"Step away from the controls," he said.

She stared at him. His mouth was a thin line, his eyes narrow. His hand didn't shake at all.

For all her planning, she hadn't counted on this.

"I mean it, Hallie," he said. "Step away from those controls."

She raised her chin ever so slightly, and said, "Did I tell you I was raised in Vallevu?"

His expression didn't change. His hand remained steady. "So?" he asked.

"Do you even know what that means?" she asked.

"It means I'm supposed to ask 'How many people did you lose?'" he said, "and you're supposed to tell me that you lost a husband or a boyfriend or a parent and how awful it was, not knowing if they were really dead or not. I'm supposed to express sympathy, and understanding of all you went through, and—"

She leaned backwards, nearly falling, and at the very last second, turned so that she made sure she hit the right controls. The entire base shook, which she hadn't expected, although she should have, because rockets were zooming out of the side of the building, heading to Palmyra, to Desierto Amarillo, to that stupid research site, which was really a backup site for the evil that was stealth tech.

And through it all, he didn't shoot her. He didn't do anything.

She turned back around.

"I lost my entire family," she said. "*And* all the adults who worked at the space station. *And* a lot of friends, and parents of friends. I lost a community, horribly, and some people *still* think that those who disappeared in that stealth tech 'experiment' will come back one day, but you and I know that if they do, they'll be mummified or worse, alive for a half second because the Empire destroyed the station, did you know that? So if they do return because of the time properties of the misused tech, they'll arrive without environmental suits in orbit. And they're not the only ones who've died using the tech. They're not even the only ones who've died horribly because of the tech. They're—"

"Spare me," he said. "You just murdered forty innocent people."

"They were working on stealth tech," she said.

"They were working on the effects of space travel on those raised in gravity," he said. "They had no idea that the backup site for stealth tech research existed below their facility."

"So what?" she asked.

"So that's murder," he said. "What you just did. It's murder."

She smiled at him. She really wasn't concerned with his dubious morality. She had told him that in the past, and her view hadn't changed.

"So what are you going to do?" she asked. "Arrest me?"

"No," he said, and fired.

2

HE WAS WATCHING THE WOMAN, because no one else seemed to be. Yves Beltraire stood, hands clasped behind his back, in his own command center—as he liked to think of the tiny side office Edward Quintana had given him. Beltraire had screens running on three walls, covering every inch of it. The ceiling was black, with some ambient light floating down. He liked letting the light from the screens around him illuminate this space.

Beltraire stood because he hated sitting. Sitting made a man stupid, and unable to respond quickly to whatever the latest challenges were.

He didn't know what the latest challenges would be; he just knew there would be some.

His entire life was about challenges.

He had the woman on only one screen, right in the center of the screens on the back wall. She bothered him, this Rosealma Quintana. She was Edward Quintana's ex-wife, but no one else seemed to know or care.

That was the problem with nicknames. People did not make the proper connections. Everyone on this research station—one of the largest in the Enterran Empire—knew Edward Quintana as Quint. If they had ever learned his last name, they had long since forgotten it.

And as for hers, they were so blinded by her résumé that they didn't seem to care about the large gaps in it.

Beltraire cared about the gaps. And the relationship. And all the details about Rosealma Quintana that no one else seemed to know. She seemed a little too intense, a little too focused. Her work history made no sense either.

Offered the position as Director of Stealth Tech for the entire Empire, and she turned it down only to bounce around the Empire. Getting a medical degree that she never formally used, ultimately diving with a tourist diving company that also did salvage. Notifying the Empire of a damaged Dignity Vessel before returning to a place called Vallevu to volunteer as their on-site medic, until she vanished one day.

Quint said she went to work in the Nine Planets Alliance before coming back to the Empire, coming back to one of the most top-secret research facilities *in* the Empire. Quint seemed only mildly bothered by that, which wasn't like him. Usually Quint kept track of every detail of every person he suspected of something on board this station.

Quint didn't seem to care about what this woman did. And she did a lot. She handled everything here. She touched the experiments, she placed her hands on tabletops, she investigated side pockets of offices that weren't even hers.

Even Beltraire wasn't cleared to go into some of those offices. He needed permission from Quint, and every time he asked Quint for the ability to physically check on this woman, this Rosealma Quintana, Quint would get a small, mysterious smile on his face.

"She's fine," he would say.

Beltraire had never thought Quint was the kind of man whose infatuation with a woman would overtake his common sense, but apparently it had.

So Beltraire was watching her, recording her, and keeping track of her every move.

And those every moves, he believed, made her highly suspicious.

He'd been watching her this afternoon, and his suspicions were growing. She had taken some supplies from her office to the *Dane*, the personal cruiser she had arrived in.

He had surreptitiously scanned everything she had taken out of the research station. He wasn't sure what he was looking for—information, maybe, or something worse, but he wasn't finding anything except clothing, shoes, and some fresh food items.

More like supplies for a trip, which he did not see logged into the travel request forms. He would use all of that to discuss her behavior with Quint.

Again.

Beltraire shifted, scanning the other images on all of the screens. They showed various sites around the station, places where Rosealma Quintana had gone, other secure areas that required four-hour reviews from human eyes despite the 24-hour monitoring.

He was beginning to feel like a glorified security guard, rather than the second-in-command for Imperial Intelligence on this extremely important research site.

What the scientists here did not understand was that his education was as good as theirs or maybe better. Sure, he didn't have one specialty that would have narrowed his focus and—in his personal, rarely expressed, opinion—also would have narrowed his mind. His mind was large enough to grasp almost anything, and he could grasp what was being researched here beyond the basics, although more than one scientist here didn't believe he could understand that.

Beltraire understood not only the concepts, and often how the scientists arrived at the hypotheses that they were trying to prove, but he also understood the real-life applications for these experiments. He—and Quint, most likely—would be the first to put some of these experiments into practice.

Beltraire saw patterns, and because he saw patterns, he knew something was off with Rosealma Quintana. Something that seemed dangerous, something that would come back to bite the entire station if she wasn't stopped.

He unclasped his hands and sighed. She was on her ship at the moment, and when she got off of it, she would probably return to her office. If he was going to speak to Quint—again—then he needed to do so now.

Beltraire turned toward the door when something on one of the screens caught his eye. The screen from the Desierto Amarillo had gone blank. He had focused so long on Rosealma Quintana that he wasn't sure when the images from the desert had disappeared.

He pulled out the drawer filled with the computer system connected to the research station in Desierto Amarillo. The desert, which covered most of a continent on Palmyra, was as far from here as possible while still remaining inside the Empire. That was by design.

The research station in Desierto Amarillo was large, but mostly for show. The kind of research it did was mostly unconnected to the research here, which focused primarily on stealth tech. There, at the Desierto Amarillo facility, they worked on the effects of space travel on those raised in gravity, as well as some other things Beltraire didn't care about.

What he did care about was what ninety percent of the Desierto Amarillo research station was used for: backup for the research done here. Everything there was to know about stealth tech lived underground at that facility. Plus, all the current research, the things that the Empire still was trying to learn about stealth tech, lived at that station.

It wasn't the only backup for this facility. There were four others, scattered around the Empire, most of them as far away from here as the Desierto Amarillo facility. They were classified top secret. Not even the researchers who worked there knew what was backed up beneath the main building.

Beltraire stared at the empty screen for a moment, feeling annoyed. He would have to deal with this, and he didn't want to. The feed from the Desierto Amarillo facility had failed more than any other feed. The problem was the weather. The heat did not mix well with the equipment that the Empire had placed in the desert itself.

Beltraire leaned over, pulled out the keyboard attached to that system, and punched in a few commands to toggle to one of the inside feeds. He didn't care about what the researchers were doing; he wanted to see the backups below the surface.

He opened three different windows on his screen: one to show the flow of the backup between this station and the one on Desierto Amarillo; another to show a visual image of one of the lower levels; and a third to show the main floor research station, where the scientists worked on the research particular to that site.

But Beltraire couldn't get any reading at all from the last two. No images from the lower level, and none from the main floor.

He pulled another keyboard out and keyed in commands so that he could see if the security systems were down on that level. The screen came up gray, which he had never seen before. He hadn't seen anything like any of this before.

Usually he got some kind of reading, something that told him what the problem was. He wasn't getting anything at all.

He looked back at the original screen—the one he had divided into three windows. Two of the windows were still black, as if they were getting no information.

But the first one, the one that showed files flowing from this station to the station on Desierto Amarillo, was full of activity. He had to isolate the activity, though, before he understood it.

The files were flowing from here to Desierto Amarillo, but couldn't find a host nodule. They couldn't find any point of contact at all.

So, like they were designed to do, the files flowed back to this station and got stored in a larger node, so that they would be resent when everything came back up.

He stared at that for a long moment. He knew this particular failsafe existed—he recommended that there be two of them—but he had never seen it function before.

Something had to go really wrong to make all the systems go down at once. All five of the backup sites had redundancies upon redundancies upon redundancies. The power systems weren't linked up. The nodes were separated. The security systems even used different underlying technology. Even if they shut down, the backup system shouldn't have.

A small shiver ran down his back. He didn't like this. But before he initiated any of the protocols or contacted Quint, Beltraire needed to check a few other things.

First, he pulled out keyboards connected to the screens showing the remaining backup sites. He needed to make sure that what he was seeing from those sites was actually what was happening there. So he went through the checklist on each visual, making sure it was a real-time image (or as close to real time as he could get).

They came back clean.

The only problem was at the Desierto Amarillo site.

That eased his mind a bit. He was worried that there was some problem here, on this research station.

It showed him how very paranoid he was about Rosealma Quintana. He had somehow thought that maybe she had gone after the backup feeds.

But if she had, wouldn't the feed be stopped at the source, not trying to contact the Desierto Amarillo site? Or was there some trigger in the system that he didn't know about, something that would set off alarms here if the information was stopped from here?

That would be something he needed to investigate. But first, he needed to finish this part of his double-check.

He moved back to the keyboard connected to the images coming (or not coming) from the Desierto Amarillo site, and keyed in commands to go back twenty-four hours.

He had that image appear in a fourth window. It took only a second or two to get the image he wanted—the image he expected.

The facility looked like a dune in the yellow desert sand, covered with some scraggly greenish yellow plants. Only if he toggled in closer could he see the main doors underneath a rocky overhang.

The overhang had been built specifically for the site. The location had been excavated, then the footprint for the building reinforced all the way down, then covered with yet another building footprint, so that the casual workers there wouldn't know what was beneath.

Then the top part of the building had been assembled, and it was small, comparatively speaking. The research area of that station could fit in a quarter of one of the floors in one of the wings here.

He let out a breath, and scanned forward as he had been taught. The image remained unchanged mostly, although a wind did come up about twelve hours in. The blowing dust made the image difficult to see from one angle, so he moved to a different one. The ability to do that was one of the many things he liked about this system.

He could still see the swirling dust, but the new angle was closer to the door. A handful of scientists moved in and out, all in ten times the normal speed, making them seem ridiculous. They didn't live onsite. Most of them lived at a base nearby, and many of them took an underground train back and forth. Only a handful came to the surface.

Some of those people lived in a nearby town with families, and had been connected to the research facility for decades rather than a few years of heavy-duty research.

He was beginning to think he would find nothing—that the images would just wink out due to some technical error—when the yellow sand blasted the camera, and then buried it, destroying the image he had been looking at.

He had no idea how that happened. The cameras were small, barely the size of a fingernail—and they were only that big because they had be quickly and easily located.

Then the image simply shut down. No yellow sand, no texture, no nothing.

He frowned, backed up the imagery, and went back to the first angle he'd been looking at. The wind had died down earlier, leaving the front of the building covered with tiny dunes that someone or something would have to shovel out.

As he had that thought, the dunes slowly diminished—something, then, which made sense. There had to be equipment to deal with those winds. And then, as he watched, a white blur streaked straight down from above, hit dead center in the scraggly bushes, and vanished.

He frowned at it. He had no idea what the blur was. He moved his right hand to slow down the imagery to run at real time, so he could see what that blur really was—when suddenly, the entire top of the base rose straight up, scraggly plants, rock outcropping and all, and then fell straight down, disappearing entirely.

He leaned forward, and as he did, sand covered that camera too, just before the camera winked out.

He cursed, his mouth dry. Had the backup research station just imploded? Or rather, had it imploded an hour or two ago? And if it had, why had no one at that town—what the hell was the name of that town?—contacted anyone here?

He pulled out another keyboard, only this one connected to a satellite above Palmyra. The satellite was in a stationary orbit over the planet, always focusing on the base.

But there was no satellite. None that he could find. So he scrolled to a secondary satellite, one that was supposed to monitor the entire planet for changes. The Empire had those satellites above every planet where critical research got done, something he had initially opposed because he figured that would make these locations easy to find, but something he suddenly understood the wisdom of.

He looked at the imagery coming from that satellite, as well as its telemetry, and saw that it was approaching the original satellite.

Only that satellite wasn't there. In its place were small bits of debris, fanning outward, as pieces were starting to move in their own orbit of the planet. Some of those pieces—the heavier ones—would slowly get pulled into the gravity well of the planet, but the others would continue floating for who knows how long.

He needed to review the imagery from the other satellite—and he hoped to hell that it had backups from the main satellite—although he doubted it did.

From here, he couldn't reposition the cameras on the second satellite to look at Desierto Amarillo. So, all he did was scan backwards until he hit the three-hour window before that white blur showed up on the research station's camera.

And then he saw it: two dozen white streaks, heading down to the surface.

His heart pounded, and his mouth was dry. He had a hunch now why he hadn't heard from the town outside the research station. He doubted the town still existed.

It was probably destroyed about the time the research station was destroyed.

But he needed to do the work before he had a firm conclusion.

He needed to know what really happened, before he brought it all to Quint.

But he couldn't take a lot of time. Because if someone (Rosealma Quintana?) had found that remote research station, had they (she) found the others? And if they (she) had, were they (was she) going to destroy them too?

His fingers actually shook as he made sure he was looking at real-time feeds from the other locations. He was. He had double-checked that before, and he triple-checked it now.

They were all right at the moment.

But he couldn't guarantee their safety much longer.

He needed to work quickly.

And he needed to keep the work quiet.

For now.

3

LUPE ETHENI'S HANDS WERE SHAKING. She cupped one of the devices in her left hand, squeezing her fist tight to make sure she didn't drop anything. The devices were of her own design, and right now she was cursing herself for making them so tiny that she could easily drop them and not realize she had done so until she needed it.

Sweat covered her entire body, even though it was cool in this control room. The room was narrow and filled with little information packets, the kind that needed to be pulled out of the wall.

She used to think those were a technological miracle, and then she started to work at Lost Souls Corporation in the Nine Planets. She saw technology—technology that was 5,000 years old—and yet it was ten, twenty, maybe a hundred times more advanced than the tech here in the Empire.

That new (old?) tech had enabled her to make these devices, which no one in the Empire should be able to detect.

Still, she felt like someone was watching her, even though she knew no one was. These remote backup stations didn't have human reviewers of security footage, so there was nothing to flag her behavior as suspicious.

And, unlike some of her colleagues on this mission, she wasn't barging into this facility. She had worked here for months, not as a scientist, but as an intern, which had been harder than she thought.

It meant she had to control her mouth, and couldn't make suggestions that would facilitate the research. And she most certainly couldn't explain to anyone here what they were doing wrong.

They didn't have the benefit of Fleet technology, like she did. They had no idea that the Fleet even existed.

She wiped her forehead with the back of her hand. She had never experienced nervous sweat before. It was accompanied by a dry mouth and that trembling. If she did this wrong, she would die.

So would everyone else on this station.

She wasn't going to do this wrong.

She kept that left fist closed tightly. She pulled open one of the drawers, saw the glowing, blinking, working parts.

It looked to her like everything in here was built backwards and ineptly, based on science that was centuries old, even though it was based on the current level of research here in the Empire, and was considered cutting edge.

For that reason, she was going beyond the assigned duties that Squishy had given her. Etheni was pulling information out of the backups, information she would take back to the Lost Souls Corporation, so that they would know exactly what the Empire was up to.

If she got caught, she could swallow the tiny devices she had pulled from these drawers, or she could stomp them to pieces before anyone could use them.

Not, as she had told her companion, Luther Cleta, that anyone here had the technology to even use the devices. But in an excess of caution, she would destroy the devices anyway.

Luther was outside the station, keeping warm in their boat. The station was on a large island in the Seltaana Sea. The sea covered two thirds of the planet Klione. The remaining third held the planet's two continents, one of which was so highly populated that buildings rose a minimum of forty stories in the air. The other was hostile to most life, due to the weather extremes.

The islands were isolated, and had been used for top-secret bases almost since the Empire was founded. They had housed this research backup station in an old research station far from the population centers.

Which was one reason why she wasn't worried—or shouldn't have been worried—about what she was going to do. The loss of life would be minimal.

Only a handful of people manned this station at any one time, and most lived off-island. Should something go really wrong, they wouldn't be harmed.

Still, a few would die. That was inevitable. She swallowed against her dry throat, wincing at the pain.

She had made some decisions that ran contrary to what Squishy wanted. Squishy wanted all of the saboteurs—and that was Etheni's word, not Squishy's—to make sure no lives were lost on this mission. But if Etheni did that, she wouldn't be able to complete the mission properly. She would have to do something—like pull an alarm or circumvent the day-to-day management system so that everyone would leave not just the station, but the island itself.

She had investigated it, more than once. And the conclusion she had come to was harsh: If she set off an alarm or changed the day-to-day operation, those in charge would get suspicious and start tracking her. Once they tracked her, she wouldn't be able to get anything done. They would mark her as a troublemaker and force her to leave.

That was the one thing Squishy hadn't realized with all of her careful planning; this backup station was so small and had so few personnel that the moment something changed, they would know who to blame.

They would blame Etheni, and then they'd kick her out of here. Or imprison her. Or call Imperial Intelligence, which was ever so much worse.

She pressed her fingers hard against her left palm, pushing the remaining device into her skin. One more piece. One more tiny piece, and then she had to leave.

She had thought it would be easy. The math worked, and she was always good at math. Math usually comforted her. Here the equation was a simple one: the number of lives saved over time versus the number of lives lost now.

The number of lives lost here in this station was three. Not even enough to rate a percentage—a realistic percentage—of the lives already lost to the Empire's seriously flawed stealth tech research.

The problem was…she blinked, feeling a lump rise in her throat. The problem was…she had met those three. Worked with them. Laughed with them (however much she tried not to). Liked them.

Even if she pulled them off the island now, Luther would kill them. He had agreed to her plan. And, logically, it was a good one.

She just had to finish executing it.

She took a deep breath, squared her shoulders, and then used her right hand to make sure the drawer was open as far as it could be. Then she peered inside and found the backup device she had placed in it. That device was almost as tiny as the device pressing into her left palm.

She removed the backup device and put it in the tiny case that rested on the small table beside her. She had set out the case at the start of this afternoon's work, and at the time, the case had been empty. Now, with the addition of that last backup device, the case was full.

She snapped the case closed and stuck it in her right pants pocket. Then she wiped her right hand on her pants. Her palm left a sweat stain on the fabric.

She tried to ignore that, and all that it meant. She didn't want to think about all she was going to do. She just needed to do it.

She took a deep breath, then bent over ever so slightly, and peered inside that drawer.

Its setup was no different than the setup in the other drawers that she had pulled open, all of them in tiny narrow control rooms like this one, all of them cool and dark and operating quietly and efficiently, as they had for years.

One last device. One more.

She could back out right now.

The thought sent a jolt of anger through her. She wasn't a quitter. She believed in this mission. She was willing to die for it. She had pledged that to Squishy, who had told her that if they did it right, death was unnecessary.

If they did it right.

Etheni braced the back of her shaking left hand on the edge of the drawer. That maneuver stopped the shaking. She slowly opened her fingers and saw the device, small and black, the size of an eyelash—a particularly short eyelash—resting between her middle and ring fingers.

She placed her right index finger over the device and flipped her hand over, so that the device wouldn't fall off. Then she slid it, very carefully, into the drawer, placing the device on top of one of the small power sources.

The device looked so innocuous there. Like a bit of dirt on top of a necklace. But the device was made with the Fleet's nanobit technology, and the moment that device touched the power source, it adhered.

She wouldn't be able to remove it, even if she wanted to.

And now that it was in place, she wasn't sure she wanted to. She slowly closed the drawer, hearing it snap shut, and then she checked her palms and fingers, just to make sure that she had done the work properly.

She had.

She let out a small sigh, then surveyed the room that would not exist an hour from now.

She nodded once and backed out, determined to walk quickly but calmly to the waiting boat.

She needed to get as far away from this island as possible.

She needed to escape.

4

EDWARD QUINTANA ARRIVED in his office first. He hated offices, rarely used them, preferring to walk the corridors of the research center. He also peered into security feeds, and occasionally surprised the scientists working at the station. Mostly, though, he'd been checking in on Rosealma.

Her presence intrigued and saddened him. She had been a lot more predictable than he wanted her to be. He had released information that several scientists had died in a stealth tech accident, and hoped it would lure her away from the work she was doing at a place called Lost Souls.

It had lured her away. She had doctored her résumé a little, leaving off Lost Souls, but everything else was true. Once upon a time, the Empire had believed in her so much that it tried to put her in charge of stealth tech.

She had turned it down, and Quint had tried to change her mind. She had yelled at him, called him—well, what she had called him he didn't like thinking about. He had thought scientists were rational beings, people who understood that occasionally the government needed to sacrifice lives in order to save lives.

Her experiments had caused deaths. That last, in the research station above Naha that housed Vallevu, the town where she and he had last lived together, had cost more lives than he liked. Than anyone liked, really.

But it had moved the research forward. Her discoveries had moved the research forward.

And then she had left.

She had moved on with her life. She hadn't come back until he released that information, and then she had shown up here, the site of the latest accident, like an avenging angel.

Only he wasn't quite sure how she was going to avenge these deaths. She really hadn't avenged the others. She had simply withdrawn, moved out of stealth tech, taken that brilliant mind and used it on something lesser. A medical degree.

And then, when she decided that wasn't enough for her, she had accompanied one of her more mysterious friends into the Nine Planets, where they did some kind of research he didn't entirely understand.

At some point, he would ask her. At some point, he would do his best to understand what she was doing now.

But that point wasn't here.

Right now, he had to deal with Beltraire.

Beltraire, who seemed to believe that Rosealma was going to destroy this station and murder thousands of people.

Quint had tried to tell him—repeatedly—that murder wasn't in Rosealma's nature, but Beltraire didn't believe him.

Beltraire was going to stop her, which Quint didn't want to do. He wanted to catch her in the act of…what?…some kind of theft?…whatever she was planning and then he wanted to pick that brilliant brain of hers, to see what was so compelling about the work occurring in the Nine Planets.

Something held Rosealma's attention, and when something science-based held her attention, that something was worth everyone's time.

He just had to figure out what it was. And he had already put her on her guard by surprising her with his presence. He should have called her into his office, talked to her, and reminded her that they once had something. Or maybe reminded her how much he respected her.

Instead, he had talked to her shortly after she had arrived, springing his presence on her as if daring her to flee.

No one had ever said that their relationship had been a healthy one.

Although Yves Beltraire had hinted at it. Beltraire was the number-two guy here, and he was angling for Quint's job. Beltraire was the smartest person Quint had ever worked with inside of Imperial Intelligence.

Unlike so many others who worked in the Imperial secrecy cadre, Beltraire made a point of learning everything he could about the area where he was assigned. Not just the personalities or the security measures, not just the general area of the research, but he delved into the research itself.

And he found stealth tech particularly intriguing.

He also believed that Rosealma was a saboteur and wouldn't listen when Quint repeated over and over again that she would never kill anyone.

It actually irritated Quint that Beltraire didn't believe him. Quint had known Rosealma better than anyone ever had, and even though Beltraire insisted that people changed, he was wrong about Rosealma.

No one changed on the most fundamental level of who they were. And at her core, Rosealma believed in preventing deaths, not causing them.

She wanted nothing to do with Quint after he had proclaimed some deaths necessary.

If he had it to do all over again, he would never have had that conversation with her. He would have let his views remain unstated, and hoped that she had understood.

Maybe he could have repaired the relationship then. There was no repairing it now.

There was a single knock on the door to his office, before it opened and Beltraire walked in. He was tall and lanky, his movements loose and seemingly unguarded, as if he were more of a boy than a man.

His face was unlined and his eyes a startling blue, a color Quint had never seen in anyone before. And in someone with skin as dark as Beltraire's, that blue made his entire face seem like it was lit from within.

It made him memorable, which Quint didn't like. He believed anyone working Intelligence needed to fade into the background.

Yet, even with those eyes, Beltraire could disappear into a room. His eyes were recessed in his face more than most people's were, and he had learned how to use his eyelids and exceptionally long eyelashes to hide those blue eyes, without using any artificial method of hiding that spectacular color.

That's what made the eyes even more impressive when they focused on someone. They seemed like they were a lot more penetrating than they should have been.

Beltraire usually projected an air of confidence and calm, but there was nothing calm about him right now. The color in his cheeks was high, his mouth was a thin line, and those startling eyes caught Quint's, and held them.

"It's safe in here?" Beltraire asked.

"Safe?" Quint repeated. Beltraire was already farther down a mental path than Quint.

"You've checked to make sure no one is listening in?" That seemed unusually paranoid for Beltraire. He knew the procedures here; that the checks occurred weekly.

But he was probably still worried about Rosealma, thinking she had done something.

She hadn't even been near Quint's office. *That* he had checked, and so far, she had stayed as far away from him as possible.

"I checked this morning," Quint said, which was the truth. He changed up the added security every week, so no one could figure out when he performed any accepted maintenance.

"Good." Beltraire pushed on the door, making sure it was closed. "We lost one of the backup sites."

Quint frowned. He had expected another conversation about Rosealma. He knew that Beltraire had been monitoring her, a bit excessively in Quint's opinion, which he had let Beltraire know more than once.

It took a half second for Quint to mentally pivot.

"Where?" he asked.

"Desierto Amarillo," Beltraire said. "Someone bombed it from orbit."

Quint blinked again, feeling as if the floor of the station had shifted underneath his feet.

"And the bombs went deep," Beltraire said. "The station didn't explode. It imploded."

Quint let out a breath. That meant that everything inside that station had been destroyed.

"Deaths?" he asked, because that was what he would be asked first by his superiors.

"I don't know yet," Beltraire said. "But if I were going to take out a backup station, it wouldn't be that one. I didn't think anyone outside of Imperial Intelligence and the handful of people who worked there knew about that research station. It was well hidden. There are others that aren't."

He was right. The research station in Desierto Amarillo wasn't obvious to anyone. It wasn't even visible to the naked eye. The aboveground research didn't give off any unusual energy signatures. The unusual energy signatures were buried deep, belowground. Undetectable, as far as the Empire was concerned.

The Empire and its equipment. The unusual energy signatures were always a surprise to anyone who got extremely close to certain parts of the aboveground location. And, from above, the heat signatures were masked by the desert.

The Desierto Amarillo station was one of the last backup stations built. As Imperial Intelligence got more and more involved with the plans, the stations became harder and harder to detect.

Perhaps the easiest one to detect was the one on Klione. That station had been there so long that everyone in the region knew of its existence. If someone were protesting the backup stations, or the research, or was trying to get the Empire's attention, the Klione facility was the one to target.

But because the Empire knew that station's vulnerabilities, it monitored that station well, particularly from orbit.

Beltraire had longer to consider this information than Quint did. Beltraire knew all the ins and outs of the various backup stations, and it had brought him to Quint. Which meant that Beltraire believed something nefarious was going on.

"What do you think is happening?" Quint asked.

"I don't know, but if someone wants to take out our research, then hitting the backup stations is the first order of business."

Beltraire didn't have to say Rosealma, because they both knew that was who he meant. They had had too many discussions about Rosealma already, and part of that was Quint's fault. He hadn't been honest with Beltraire, hadn't told him that he was luring Rosealma out of hiding in the Nine Planets with planted information.

Quint probably should have told Beltraire that, but it was too late now. Now, it would seem like a justification. They'd argued about her too much for Beltraire to ever believe Quint on the topic of Rosealma again.

Quint let silence hang between them for a moment, using that silence as a way of having that conversation yet again, a conversation he always shut down anyway.

"You think this isn't targeted at the research going on aboveground at Desierto Amarillo," Quint said. It wasn't quite a question, because he didn't think it was the aboveground research either.

Beltraire gave him a withering look. "I don't think we can afford to assume that."

"I agree," Quint said.

Beltraire leaned backwards ever so slightly, as if Quint's words surprised him.

"We'll treat this like the sabotage it is, and also assume that every single backup site has been targeted," Quint said.

"There's no reason to target them without targeting the main research sites," Beltraire said. "Like here."

"I've been monitoring it," Quint said. "So far, there hasn't been a lot of suspicious activity."

"Except for Rosealma," Beltraire said. Apparently he had to get that into the conversation.

Quint nodded, deciding to give Beltraire that. "Except for Rosealma," Quint said. "And even what she's doing seems to be minor. I suspect this is a different plan, but we won't know until we investigate."

"I don't think we have time," Beltraire said. "We need to protect the other sites. I'd like to request small squadrons around each facility."

Quint frowned. Something about that idea bothered him. And then he realized what it was.

"If whoever did this has discovered the Desierto Amarillo site, but not the others," he said, "then sending squadrons to all the other sites, including this one, would call attention to these places."

Beltraire opened his mouth to protest, but Quint didn't let him talk.

"In fact," Quint said quickly. "Doing so would confirm the locations of all the backup sites. It might be exactly what the saboteurs want."

Beltraire closed his mouth and pressed his lips together as if holding back the words. He looked away, shaking his head slightly.

Quint couldn't tell if Beltraire disagreed with him or if Beltraire hadn't thought of that detail and was berating himself.

"I think we order all the remaining backup sites to use emergency procedures," Quint said, "and we send in a few fighters, just to keep an eye on the orbit. Then if we see anything, anything at all, we send in a squadron."

Beltraire nodded his head just once. A quick bob that showed he agreed. He also knew how dangerous and unusual such a plan was.

Emergency procedures meant that the backup sites would have to send information—the latest first—off-site. Quint didn't like doing it because the secondary backups were extremely vulnerable to discovery. The information wouldn't have the layers of encryption that were used between this station and the regular backup sites.

But Quint saw no other choice.

"I've already scanned the areas and information around the other sites," Beltraire said, "and, aside from here, I saw suspicious activity at only one other site."

Clearly, he couldn't let the decision about Rosealma slide.

But Quint decided to ignore that.

"Where?" he asked.

"The Zargasa site," Beltraire said.

Now it was Quint's turn to be surprised. The Zargasa Research Station was almost as well hidden as the Desierto Amarillo site. The Zargasa station was located in a box valley in one of the highest mountain ranges in the entire Empire. The main part of the station protruded out of the mountain onto the valley floor, but the rest of the station went deep inside the mountain. Inside, and down.

He was beginning to understand why Beltraire thought this might be sabotage. If the Zargasa site and the Desierto Amarillo site were targeted first, that meant that they had been found using nontraditional means. In other words, someone had leaked the information.

There was no other way to discover both sites at the same time.

A thread of annoyance ran through Quint. He had opened most of the files here at the station to Rosealma, but he had also monitored her every communication and all of her actions. She hadn't looked up the backup sites, and even if she had, it wouldn't have mattered.

She hadn't contacted a soul off-station.

She hadn't even been near any communications sent off the station during the entire time she had been here.

And while she had taken supplies to her aptly named ship, the *Dane*, those supplies hadn't had any technical component at all. He knew because he had checked them himself.

He had been letting himself into and out of the *Dane* much too often. But Rosealma hadn't noticed or, if she had, she hadn't said anything.

"What's going on at Zargasa?" Quint asked Beltraire.

"Equipment malfunctions," he said. "They started about the time that the Desierto Amarillo site was attacked."

Equipment malfunctions happened often, especially at remote sites, but they usually didn't get the attention of someone like Beltraire. And Beltraire was right: equipment malfunctions at the same time as an attack on another backup site was suspicious.

"Have you let anyone on Zargasa know what you suspect?" Quint asked.

"I thought I should check with you first," Beltraire said. "I know we should have someone embedded there, but we don't that I can find."

29

The backup sites weren't important enough to waste a good agent on. Quint had never fought that decision from his higher-ups. He knew how hard training was, and how many resources it used. It was always better to put a highly trained agent where they would actually do some good, instead of wasting them on a place that hadn't seen any problems in decades.

Until now.

"We don't have anyone there," Quint said. "And before you ask, we don't have agents at any of the backup sites. That decision was made long before I got certified."

He realized how defensive that sounded. He had always thought that a chancy decision, but he had never spoken up against it.

"I don't even know who to contact there," Quint said. "Most of the researchers on-site know nothing about the backups. They think that the area where they work is all that there is to the research station."

He sighed softly. He wished he had a simpler solution than the one he was about to propose.

Beltraire frowned at him.

"How long will it take you to get there?" Quint asked.

"A day, maybe, depending on the ship and whether or not you want me to travel with someone," Beltraire said.

"You can pilot an FTL vessel, right?" Quint asked. He thought he knew the answer, but he never trusted his memory on things like this.

"Yes," Beltraire said.

"Then get there as fast as you can. I'll make sure you have fighters backing you up." Quint would have preferred that Beltraire stay here and monitor the other backup sites, but that wouldn't work right now. Quint couldn't send someone else without bringing them up to speed, and he had a sense that time was of the essence here—provided something really was going wrong.

"You want me to go alone?" Beltraire asked. He didn't sound nervous about it. He was just clarifying.

"Yeah," Quint said. And then, because he couldn't resist, he added, "Let's hope this is exactly what it looks like—equipment malfunctions that mean nothing."

"Yeah, let's hope," Beltraire said. But he didn't sound convinced.

Quint wasn't convinced either. Something was going terribly wrong. He just wasn't sure—yet—what exactly that something was.

5

NOTHING HERE WAS LIKE IT WAS SUPPOSED TO BE. The specs for the Zargasa station were all wrong. Darya Koh had spent the last three months working her butt off, trying to learn the new system.

She had assigned her guardian and protector, Enan Noor, to find the entrances to the backup sections of the research station, which turned out to be a tougher task than expected.

Both Koh and Noor managed to get hired on here. Noor worked security, which allowed him to check doors and security systems, and Koh found work as an intern, mostly by pretending to know a lot less than she did.

That had been Squishy's plan for all of them—that they work at the facilities before destroying them. Squishy had believed that they would have a greater chance of learning the systems that way, and of making certain that no one got harmed when the backup station was destroyed.

Koh hadn't been certain it would work—she had initially believed she was not a good enough actress to handle undercover work—but all she had to do was channel the insecurities she had had when she was an actual intern. Oh, and tap into the insecurities she had at the moment.

Insecurities that were getting worse by the second. Because she was now deep inside the backup site, way back in the mountain, and she wasn't exactly sure what she was doing.

Noor was guarding the entrance to the entire backup site. If some-one came toward them or tried to contact security, he would know. If it looked like someone had figured out what Koh was doing, then Noor would be the one to take her into custody, and Noor would get her out of this godforsaken valley, which she hoped she would never see again.

She was trying not to be claustrophobic. She hadn't realized she *was* claustrophobic until she started to work here. She wasn't claustrophobic on spaceships or in tight spaces on space stations. She'd never experi-enced anything quite like what she was feeling here.

She wasn't even certain claustrophobic was the right word.

She could mentally feel the weight of the entire mountain pressing down on her. The deeper she went, the more her heartrate spiked.

She was terrified of being trapped down here, of getting buried under hundreds and hundreds and hundreds of feet of rock and debris.

Some of this, she suspected, was because she was going to destroy everything down here, and that might cause rooms and tunnels to collapse.

But she was setting everything on a timer, and she knew exactly when the collapse would happen.

At least she had designed the timer. And the explosives. They were dainty little things, not anything someone from the Empire would rec-ognize. All of the tech here was ancient and clunky and counterintui-tive. She had to try Empire tech three different times just to get it to work right.

Which was making her worry right now. She had tripped a few dif-ferent alarms and managed to shut them down, typing in—*typing!*—that she was dealing with a maintenance problem. But she had no idea if that was red-flagging her work or not.

She needed to be finished quickly. She was putting an explosive device on each level—it wasn't really fair to call them floors. There were no real corridors and the walls were covered with what looked like little drawers, filled with equipment. The drawers were held in place by col-umns that ran all the way to the lowest level.

She had taken an elevator down to that level, which might be why she had become so unnerved so quickly. She hadn't felt bad when she worked as an intern in the research part of Zargasa station. But the research part jutted out onto the valley floor, partly so that the offices on the side where the administrator and her team worked had real light.

The light down here was gray or brown, depending on what level she was on. No one had replaced the lights in a long time, and no one had cleaned the housing.

Even though the drawers and columns were filled with equipment, everything was coated with a fine layer of gray dust, which she found just appalling. She had no idea if that same dust was inside the equipment, but she suspected it was.

And that suspicion made her wonder if she even needed to do the work at all. Because if that fine dust got into the equipment, then the equipment wasn't functioning properly. The backups might not even exist.

When she discovered that the dust was everywhere—which was very early this morning—she considered aborting the entire mission. She knew that some of the reason she wanted to abort were the people who worked in the research section. She liked them—all of them. They were scientists with precise minds and firm ways of doing things. Some of them lacked social skills. But all of them seemed kind or at least interesting, and she valued that.

She had a plan to get them out of the station—the ones who lingered after hours. Most would go home anyway, an hour or two from now, but the rest needed to be encouraged to leave.

When she got back to the upper level, she would shut down the environmental systems, and do so in a way that wouldn't be easily repaired. When the station imploded—and it would, about an hour later—everyone would remember the loss of light and oxygen, the flashing warnings recommending an evacuation, and think it was all of a piece, not realizing that the piece had a lot more to do with her than with any kind of malfunction.

Just once Noor had asked her if she would be upset if one of her Zargasa colleagues died. Koh had thought about it, and then said that she would be upset. She had liked all of them.

But would she be devastated? Would she blame herself?

Of course not. If someone had an evacuation order, then that person needed to evacuate. If they failed, then the problem was theirs, not hers.

Maybe that made her a bit callous. But she suspected that the scientists on the first floor—rational, logical, smart, and precise—would agree with her assessment.

Sometimes there had to be loss to ensure a gain. If she could minimize the loss, she would. It was just like minimizing risk.

She would do the best she could.

That best included finding the best place to put her dainty explosives. She was doing it all on the fly right now, because she didn't have an accurate floor plan of these levels. The floor plan she had been working off of had been drawn before the station was built, and whoever had drawn them had a different vision for this section than whoever set the section up.

She didn't like winging it, but she was on a clock.

All five teams were targeting their sites today, theoretically at the same time of day. They wanted the deed done.

Squishy had said she had one other plan for that exact time of day. And then they would all meet up, get away together.

Get away clean.

Koh wasn't sure about clean. She wasn't even sure about together.

But she would do her best to be precise.

The attack was supposed to begin in an hour.

She would do everything in her power to make sure that it did.

6

THE FTL VESSEL THAT QUINT had assigned Beltraire was smaller than Beltraire wanted. It was a cruiser, built for a family or maybe a group of researchers. Except, of course, there was nowhere to research in the vessel.

And there were no weapons on board either. Which, apparently, was why Quint had said he was going to send fighters.

The fighters would meet Beltraire when he came out of FTL near Hshligt, the planet which housed Zargasa Station. The fighters had better be there, because he couldn't act without them.

This ship, called the *Minunat,* had only speed to recommend it. It had some defensive capability, the way that private ships did, with a few shields that he could have punched through with the most rudimentary Empire military vessel. The shields on this thing were there to make the customers happy, not to actually protect anyone from anything.

He was hoping he wouldn't need shields or anything else. But he had no idea what he was facing. Quint hoped that those readings were equipment malfunctions, but neither of them believed that they were.

The cruiser was long and narrow, with a point at the front end, so that it looked fast, especially in flight. It was painted a bright red, which he found amusing. It meant that the cruiser probably belonged to some scientist, and only the regulations at the research station—which claimed that any ship could be used for any purpose—allowed him to fly it to Hshligt.

If the ship got destroyed, Quint would have to answer for it, not Beltraire.

Beltraire sat in the pilot's seat. The navigation equipment ran underneath the portholes, which were extensive. He was actually surrounded by clear, reinforced windows, rather than walls.

Nothing about this ship was safe, and if he had had the time, he would have protested. But he had no real choice.

He needed to get to Zargasa Station as fast as possible.

He would shift to the stardrive in about thirty minutes. The specs for this vessel stated that it needed some run time before it could make the leap into faster-than-light travel. If he had known that, he might have taken a more functional vessel, one that couldn't run quite as fast initially, but which would get him there—with offensive and the proper kind of defensive capability.

After spending a futile few minutes trying to find a way to shield the windows around the cockpit, he finally set up his own equipment. He needed to track the other bases. He had brought sanctioned small computers, and hoped they would work on this vessel.

So far, they seemed to.

But he couldn't access the most classified information, so he sent a request to Quint, giving this ship access. Quint wanted him on this vessel after all, so Quint could give this vessel clearance.

Beltraire let out a breath, then slid deeper in the pilot's chair. He probably should explore the cruiser just to see if there were any surprises, but he didn't plan to be on it long.

Just long enough to get to Zargasa Station and see what the hell was really going on there.

And to make whatever it was stop.

7

GORKA DRAGGED CONIFER'S BODY out of the weapons room of the deserted moon base. Light gravity was still gravity, and she was heavier than he had expected.

He couldn't bring himself to carry her. He could barely bring himself to touch her.

She had fallen backwards against the weapons array, and for one brief, hopeful second, he thought maybe she had shut everything down.

But of course she hadn't. She landed on it with a thud, and then her body slipped off it and crumpled onto the floor.

Her eyes were open the entire time, and the one thing he thought as he stared at her, the thing he noticed, was that their expression never changed.

Apparently she was as sure of herself in death as she had been in life. Bitch.

She had made him and Squishy and everyone else on every other team a party to murder.

Squishy had been clear: she hadn't wanted any additional loss of life.

She had felt responsible for the deaths in that space station above Vallevu twenty-one years ago. She had been running the experiments. She hadn't foreseen what a post-doc would do, running his own experiments without checking with her, and thus destroying an entire part of the station.

Squishy had been running from that ever since. It was why she had become a doctor, and somehow, through all of that, she had partnered with Boss, who owned the Lost Souls Corporation, and there, they worked with the people who really knew how stealth tech worked, the people who had come through their own trial by fire, people who called themselves the Fleet.

Gorka had no idea how he would tell Squishy they had failed on their mission. Oh, they destroyed the stealth tech backups, and if the other teams were successful in destroying all the backups and Squishy managed to destroy the ongoing research, then the Empire's experimentation with stealth tech would be done.

So that part of the mission had been successful.

But Squishy had been clear during that last meeting, where they had gotten their assignments. They had to minimize the loss of life. They had to make sure that no one else died.

And Gorka had failed miserably at that.

He wasn't going to blame Conifer. He should have realized just how crazy she was underneath. She had been willing to sacrifice those lives all along, and he had been stupid enough to let her work on the weapons systems.

He should have focused on getting her out of there, maybe trying to complete the mission himself.

Although he didn't have the training or the expertise in engineering. He knew nearly nothing about the systems used in the Empire, and even less about the Empire's historical systems.

He couldn't have destroyed that backup station even if he wanted to. He had needed Conifer for that, and she had done it.

Five hours earlier than she was supposed to, but she had done it.

And he had let her.

He was complicit.

And if there weren't other lives at stake—all of his compatriots, the other teams that were destroying the remaining backup stations—he would stay here, let the Empire catch him, and do what they would with him.

But he didn't dare.

Because they had destroyed the station early.

That had been one of Squishy's main points: don't veer off the timeline. Because if they did, they might all get caught.

And of course, Conifer had veered off. Of course, she was going to screw this up for everyone—even though she was dead.

Maybe because she had died.

Which made him even more complicit.

It had taken him a few minutes to decide whether or not he would leave her behind. Maybe, if she had been someone else, he would have left her.

But she had been born in the Empire, and had a history here, and they probably knew she had gone to Lost Souls. They would know who was behind this, just by identifying her body.

So he couldn't leave her here.

Still, he had pushed her with the toe of his boot, half expecting her to open her eyes and say something truly nasty to him.

But she didn't.

Her expression didn't change. Her eyes didn't close. She didn't grab at him or even try to push herself up on her elbow.

He had killed her.

He holstered the laser pistol, then bent over and grabbed her ankles. They were spindly, which he hadn't expected. He felt like he could snap them just by squeezing them too hard, which made him a bit hesitant, until he realized she couldn't feel anything that he did.

He had injured people before, doing his job. He had shot people too. He had never killed anyone.

And although he felt like he should have some regret, he really didn't. He was relieved she was gone. He hadn't realized just how much her very presence irritated him.

He had pulled her along the floor, gingerly at first, and then as hard as he could. By the time he reached the door, he no longer cared about how he treated her. He just wanted her out of the base and himself along with her.

He had to take her to the ship and get her off this godforsaken moon, but he didn't have to take her all the way to the meet-up.

Once he was underway, he would toss her out the airlock.

As he pulled her through the door, her lolling head hit the frame with a meaty sound. He stopped, saw a bit of hair and gristle, thought for a moment about whether or not he should leave it, and then decided to. If the Empire found it, they found it. They might test everything, or they might just bury this whole thing.

And if they got here after all of the backup sites had been destroyed and the research station was gone, they wouldn't even care about the bits and pieces of himself and Conifer he left behind. They would be dealing with an Empire-wide crisis.

He pulled her toward the ship, wishing he could leave her.

But that wouldn't be smart.

He was beginning to think none of this was smart.

But it was much too late to change his mind.

8

HIDDEN LOCATIONS FOUND, satellites in orbit destroyed, an entire backup station gone. The others transmitting their most recent information to unsecured sites right now.

Quint let out a breath, then ran a hand through his hair. Maybe he needed to pay attention to Beltraire's suspicions. Yes, Quint knew that Rosealma was here under false pretenses, and he knew that she hadn't been in contact with anyone about anything, but—and that *but* was important—she was good at systems. She was good at figuring out how to get things done while seeming to do something else.

Had he underestimated her again?

He opened his own system, logged on, and turned on all the security feeds. He kept an eye open for Rosealma's small form. He found it, in her office, and she seemed nervous. She was rubbing her left hand on her right forearm, something she always did when she expected trouble in one form or another.

He could confront her now, or he could see what she was going to do. And he could do that while he was looking up one other thing: Her damn awful nickname, the one she had gotten when she had worked with that diving company.

People at the Lost Souls Corporation who knew Rosealma didn't call her by her given name or even by a shortened variation of it.

They called her Squishy, for reasons he couldn't quite fathom. Nothing about her even suggested that the nickname would be appropriate.

Maybe, if he looked through logs and contacts and identifications, he would find "Squishy" instead of "Rosealma" or her call numbers.

He started into the work, feeling almost like he was betraying her.

Then he stopped. That thought actually registered with him.

Betraying her.

The woman who had left him, who had thought him unworthy. The woman who condemned him for taking a practical approach to both science and the security of the Empire.

The woman who had treated him—once she had arrived here—as if he meant nothing at all.

He made himself sigh. He had lured her here so that he could find out what kind of research she had been doing at Lost Souls, and so far, he had gotten absolutely no information from her. And now he was worried because he was being sensible, and spying on her—or rather, looking into all she had been doing, more than he had looked into it before.

Truth be told, he had counted on Beltraire to keep an eye on her. Quint had known that Beltraire would see things more clearly than he would. Beltraire—rightly—hadn't trusted her.

But Beltraire was off-station now, and monitoring Rosealma was up to Quint.

He started the deep search, thinking maybe he would locate something that "Squishy" had done.

But as he let the system track her, he watched her moving her hand nervously over her arm.

"What are you up to, Rose?" he asked. "What are you trying to do?"

9

AN ICE STORM. That was just what they needed.

Dagmar Gagne bent her head into the wind, letting the pellets hit the top of her skull instead of her face. She had lost her hat half an hour ago, so she had wrapped her scarf around her head so many times that she felt almost mummified. What she wouldn't give for an environmental suit right now.

Clay Skopf was behind her. Somehow he managed to keep his hat, but he didn't have a scarf. So his face was red and ice covered, even though he had tucked as much of it as possible into the collar of his thick green coat.

They were dressed like locals because they had become locals these past six months. But she wasn't going to miss the base at Decision Heights at all.

The ice storm was the last indignity. Living on the top of a mountain, literally in the clouds at times, got old real fast. Particularly when the scientists who worked the research station made fun of the newcomers, and didn't teach them how to properly handle things like the thinner air up here.

They didn't let her bring an environmental suit to the job, preferring that everyone use the local tech, which was a combination of an Empire environmental suit (eminently inferior to the ones she'd been using in the Nine Planets) and old-fashioned cloth coated with something that withstood cold.

She had gotten used to working in the cold, since the research part of the station was always kept about ten degrees below what she (and any spaceship she'd ever served on) considered normal.

But she hadn't been outside enough, especially in snow.

And little did they know when Squishy had set the dates for the destruction that it would be the beginning of the fall here on this part of Telaan. Even though the valley floors were still experiencing something akin to summer (it never got really warm down there), the mountain ranges were now getting the periodic storms that would eventually snow all the researchers in.

Some of them—crazy idiots—were looking forward to that. Skopf had had to completely disable the environmental systems and remove any possibility of repairing the heating systems just to get the entire group to leave the base for two days. Even then, he'd had to do some fast talking to keep the engineers from getting supplies and coming right back.

Half the research team loved this place. The rest loved it even more.

Which Gagne hadn't understood at all. She had managed to clear the research site while Skopf was working on the backup systems below. He believed that the explosives he was using would take off half the mountain top, and he wanted to warn the people living in the villages below about that.

But Gagne had stopped him. Their mission was to destroy the base and make sure no one died *at the base*. If the mountain decided to be even more vicious than it already was, well, she figured they could deal with it.

The mountain wasn't an active volcano, and it seemed stable enough to her, not that she was a geologist. She wasn't any kind of "ist," really. Her job here had been to protect Skopf and get him the hell out of here when the time came.

The time should have come earlier than it did. She'd been watching this storm for days. The local forecasters knew it was coming, and she had learned to trust them. Storms formed over this mountain—which was apparently how it got its name.

The "decision" in Decision Heights referred not to any human decisions, but the meteorological decisions. The mountain somehow "helped," in local parlance, weather systems decide whether or not to form.

Apparently, they usually decided *to* form, instead of falling apart.

She wished this ice storm would fall apart. She'd never experienced anything like it, and she'd grown up in a wintry climate, lived through snowstorms and so-called blizzards.

But nothing as intense as this. The entire mountainside was a pearlescent gray. She had walked this path not three days ago, getting their ship into position so that it could launch from the protected crevice she had parked it in.

The ship was only a kilometer from the base, and it had taken her less than fifteen minutes to walk the path. No one in the research station had monitored her, and no one seemed to know that the ship existed.

She had planned that part well. This ship had Fleet-level shielding technology, which looked like a cloak to Enterran equipment. Nothing on their systems registered the ship as existing at all, except for the fact that right now, the entire thing was probably getting covered in a layer of ice.

If anyone was eyeballing it, they would see the ice forming around the shape of the ship.

But she had no idea who would eyeball it. Somehow, she and Skopf had managed to get everyone off the mountain, including the reluctant ones. And she had helped Skopf plant the last of the explosives.

They had finished with ninety minutes to spare, and then they had gathered their things, put on their gear, and headed for the trail.

She was chilled to the bone, not able to see much, and worried they would never arrive at the ship.

Skopf, to his credit, wasn't complaining. He just moved forward, head as far down as he could get it, and stayed behind her, letting her take the brunt of the wind.

She finally reached the outcropping of rocks that brought her to the crevasse where they had left the ship. She couldn't see the ship from here—she could barely see the rocks in front of her—but she knew it was off to her right, down a slight (and probably dangerous now) incline.

She braced her right hand on the rock. The ice wasn't slippery—yet, anyway. It was sticky, as if it still contained some liquid. Or maybe it was just too cold. She didn't know, and didn't have time to figure it out.

She had to wait a moment for Skopf to get close enough to see her. He waggled two fingers of his left hand, and then—gratefully, it seemed to her—gripped the rock to the right.

Then she started down the incline. After two very slippery steps, she braced her left hand on the rock outcropping on the left side, balancing herself down the narrow trail. She hoped the incline would level out before the rocks on her left widened. She couldn't remember if the incline remained steep all the way down. It had been a cold but sunny afternoon when she found this spot, just three days before.

Gagne glanced behind her, saw Skopf pick his way down, and then peered past him, just making sure no one had followed.

As far as she could tell, no one had. And if they did, they would have as many problems as she did.

She nodded at Skopf once, then kept going down, taking her time, even though they really didn't have time. This trip felt like it was taking forever, and she knew a clock was ticking. They had to get as far from this mountaintop as possible as quickly as possible, and she wasn't sure what problems she would find with the ice and snow.

The corner turned into a wide curve, and she lost her grip on the left-side rocks. But the wind wasn't as severe in here, and the ice dripped down, more like snow than driven ice pellets. Her boots still slipped against the surface, but she wasn't quite as afraid of falling.

But if she looked up, she could see the storm just a few meters overhead, the swirling ice blocking her view of the clouds above. The ice storm waited for her, threatening, and she really didn't want to experience it again.

Skopf caught up to her. He didn't stand beside her, but almost slid into her back. His face was still red, but the tip of his nose had turned white, and that was a problem that the scientists in the station had warned her about. Frostbite, something she had never experienced. She hoped the automated medical unit in the ship could help with that.

She wasn't going to tell Skopf about any of it until they got inside.

She rounded the last part of the corner, and sure enough, she could see the ship. It looked large in this small space. The ship had smooth lines and several curves of its own. It was Fleet design.

In person, the ship was visible to the naked eye, but it would be invisible—even now—to Empire sensors. The fact that the storm wasn't blowing ice into the crevasse worked to her advantage. If the ice had formed a layer over the ship, that would have been something the Empire's sensors could read. But they couldn't—not at the moment, anyway.

No one was looking for her or Skopf. None of the scientists who worked at the base even knew they were missing. No one would figure that out until the base blew, and even then, the others would probably think she and Skopf had died rather than figure out that they had set the bombs and escaped.

She made it to the ship's entrance on its right side, then punched in the code. Normally, she would have used some kind of bioscan, but in this weather, she was afraid of touching any surface with her bare hands.

The ship eased to life, lights coming on slowly, and heaving a sigh as systems started up, much like a human waking from sleep.

The door opened inward, and a ramp formed, sliding down into the bits of snow on the crevasse's floor.

She turned to Skopf. "You first," she said.

He gave her a confused look, and she couldn't decide if that was because to have him go first wasn't procedure or if it was because he was having some kind of issue because of the ice and snow and cold.

Maybe it was a combination of both. Whatever was going on with him, she needed him out of the weather as quickly as possible.

He climbed the ramp, swaying a little, as if he still felt the strong wind. The wind was above them, blowing over the crevasse, not into it, and she knew that it couldn't be affecting him. So his legs or his balance were going. Or maybe he was just exhausted from the trip here.

She would have to keep an eye on him—after she got them out of there.

She followed him up the ramp, prepared to catch him if he lost his balance and fell. He slipped inside the airlock and peered at the bioimager. It caught his face, noted the conditions, and realized that it didn't have to keep both doors closed.

So the interior door opened, and he stumbled inside just as she reached the airlock.

She paused and gave one last look to the rocks of the crevasse, the falling ice-snow, and the mountaintop. She was probably going to be the last person to see this sight. It would all be gone soon enough.

That bothered her more than she expected.

Then she shook off the feeling, turned, and entered the ship herself, the main door closing behind her.

10

QUINT FINISHED STARING AT THE BACKUP STATIONS. He wasn't seeing much out of the ordinary, and he needed to stop worrying about them. The screens were distracting him from work, anyway.

He didn't belong in his office. He needed to walk the corridors. He had some investigating to do. Before he talked to Rosealma, he wanted to know what the other scientists thought of her.

He pushed off the nearby counter and shut down the screens. Then he pushed the keyboards back into their drawers. The office returned to its narrow, sterile self, devoid of all personality, including his.

The destruction of Desierto Amarillo had left him unsettled and a little uncertain, which wasn't like him at all. He usually knew what he was going to do next and what was going to happen next. He hadn't expected the backup station to blow, though, and he didn't like what Beltraire suspected would happen next.

But Quint couldn't act until he had more information. And some of that information couldn't come from him, or from staring at screens, or even from looking at anomalies in data coming from the other backup stations.

He probably should bring the information to the station head, or maybe even to his superiors in Imperial Intelligence, but he wasn't willing to. Not yet.

Before he did, he needed to talk with Rosealma, figure out what she'd been working on, and see if she knew about the other bases. He would probably have to tip his hand, tell her what he had done, or, maybe, if he played it right, get her to confess.

When they were married, he could read her very well, even when she was lying to him—which she rarely did. But since she came here, he noticed that she was an entirely different woman, one who was guarded and measured and rarely wore her emotions on her face.

If she hadn't looked just like the Rosealma he remembered, he would have thought her a completely different woman.

Underneath it all, though, was the curious scientist and woman of strong opinions that he had known. With the right attitude, he might be able to coax that woman to the surface, and then figure out what he needed to know.

Maybe she would even tell him, if he asked directly. Maybe she wouldn't hide a thing.

Then he smiled. He doubted that would happen. She had treated him like he was the enemy ever since she had arrived.

He was about to leave the office when his inner office comm chimed. It was too soon to be Beltraire. He probably wouldn't contact Quint for several more hours, if then.

So Quint looked at the comm dash and saw that the message was coming from one of the scientists, Cloris Kashion.

Kashion had never bothered him before. He wasn't even certain she knew who he was.

Like most people on the station, she thought of him as the head of security, not as Imperial Intelligence. Maybe if she had given it some thought, she would realize that Imperial Intelligence was everywhere on this station, but he doubted she (or any of the other scientists) ever gave any thought about that.

They did their work—somewhat obliviously—and he did his, keeping track of them.

He pressed the comm button and tried to keep his voice neutral. Some of the scientists were very sensitive to tone. Too harsh, and

51

they thought he was criticizing them. Too calm, and they thought he didn't care.

"Cloris?" he asked.

She didn't appear on a screen, although he had left the visuals open. "I have found something very strange inside one of the stealth tech tubes. I was going to remove it, but I thought you should see it first."

"All right," he said. "If you turn on the screen—"

"No," she said. "You need to come here."

She didn't sound panicked, exactly, but she did sound off. Although he might have been imagining that, since he didn't know her well at all.

"I'll be right there," he said.

She hadn't given him her exact location, but he didn't need it. He opened one of the drawers and pulled out a flat screen. It was connected to the environmental system, and it showed where all the people on board were by heat signature.

Anyone could access that, but his had more detail. He could identify those signatures by name, and explore even more—to read their mood, and sometimes what they were doing.

It had taken all of his personal self-control to prevent himself from using that little technique to keep an eye on Rosealma since she had come to the station.

He finally figured out where Kashion was located. She wasn't in her research area. She was in one of the communal areas, and, oddly, she was alone.

He headed out, feeling even more unsettled than he had a moment before.

Normally, the scientists didn't contact the head of security because they had found an anomaly in one of their experiments. Normally, they figured out what caused the anomaly on their own, reported it in their research, and tried to make sure it wouldn't happen again.

She must have used the phrase "something very strange" in case anyone was listening in. Because what she was describing wasn't an anomaly, but something else.

Sabotage? Here as well as the backup sites?

He let out a sigh.

Time to bring in the entire security team.

If only he knew what to tell them to be on the watch for. Maybe he would figure that out after he spoke to Kashion and saw what she had to show him.

11

THE WHEAT FIELDS LOOKED LIKE GOLDEN WATER, waves rippling in the warm sunlight. Harini Faber found this entire region of Wuhtmu beautiful, which was a problem. She had wanted to hate it here—the pale sunlight, the bugs, the strange storms and even more unpredictable temperatures. She'd studied all of that before she came, and she had thought that she might not survive the months of preparation, of blending in.

But she was seen as yet another scientist on a mission she couldn't discuss. The nearby town of Olita was used to scientists moving in and out. They even had a dormitory for the more transitory ones.

She hadn't been able to bring herself to move into the dormitory. She hadn't wanted to get to know the various people working at the backup base, which they all thought was on the cutting edge of Empire science.

None of them had any idea that the base, hidden in the tall stalks of wheat, had two lower levels devoted to stealth tech backup. The science studied here was science she approved of—figuring out how to increase crop yields on the various planets within the Enterran Empire without harming the crops' nutrients. So much agriculture—at least the kind she was familiar with—focused on growing things in space that it ignored how to keep land-based populations fed.

She hated what she was about to do. She believed in the mission here, liked the geneticists and biologists and everyone she had met here, even the farmers who insisted on tilling some of the fields by hand, to see if the messiness of human involvement made a positive difference in plant growth, as opposed to the regimentation of machines working the land.

She stood just outside the facility with her partner, Norell Bhatt beside her. Bhatt had been another surprise. Assigned to this mission because of his tactical abilities, he'd proven to be a savvy partner, someone who understood how conflicted she was, and helped her figure out how to help.

Their plan would save lives, but it would cost all this wheat. There was no way to stop it from burning.

She took a deep breath of the fresh air. Wheat stalks had a slightly dry and tangy odor, one she had come to love.

But, she kept telling herself, wheat was replaceable. It would grow again, and maybe better, because—she had learned—fire sometimes purified or somehow improved soil.

Soil science wasn't her area of expertise. Very little of what happened here—on the surface, anyway—was in her area of expertise. But she had learned a lot.

She had even toyed with discarding the mission entirely, but that was when she learned that Bhatt would have to take over for her. And even though he agreed that lives should be protected, he did not know how to do that.

Setting up the underground level to destroy all of the backups required knowledge of computer systems and interstellar communications and the mechanics of a wide variety of explosives.

To totally destroy every bit of information inside this building, she had to destroy the building—top and bottom. Midway through this, as she infiltrated this post, she had hoped to leave the top—the agricultural side, the *innocent* side—intact.

But that would create too many mistakes. The lower level could have been saved. Parts of it might not have been obliterated. And then there were the backup procedures themselves.

She'd had to shut them down this morning, to make sure that the site didn't sense the threat and start sending backup information to one of the unsecured off-site backups.

She would have told Squishy about those if she could, but Squishy was on the main stealth tech research station and incommunicado. There was no one else to inform about the unsecured off-site backups without notifying others on the teams, also expressly forbidden.

So, she had no choice: once she left here, she and Bhatt would have to go to as many of the off-site backups as they could and destroy the information.

Those sites weren't as secure, and the information wasn't encoded. It would be vulnerable for a week, maybe more, as the Empire scrambled to figure out how to salvage its stealth tech research.

And then, if all of the teams were successful, the Empire would realize that it couldn't salvage anything.

Her heart leapt at that thought. It was the one thing that kept her going, despite her love of this location—the gorgeous wheat, the gentle and warm breeze, the kind people that surrounded her. Too many people had died already because of stealth tech research.

She'd lost her sister, her father, and her husband to a malfunctioning stealth tech field—and none of them had worked in stealth tech at all. In fact, none of them had even known what it was.

They just happened—*she* just happened—to live too close to one of the on-land ship building facilities, and there had been a mishap.

When she wasn't home. She'd been coming home from work to enjoy a dinner with all three of them—her entire family. She was bringing some wine and fresh bread from her favorite bakery. She'd stopped just a bit too long to chat with a casual friend, and when she got home—

Well, when she got home, it was fading in and out, like the rest of the neighborhood, as if the buildings themselves couldn't decide if they wanted to stay or disappear forever.

She hadn't been allowed past a perimeter that the security forces had set up, and she couldn't reach her family, no matter how hard she tried.

She thought she had seen her husband emerge from the house and gesture toward her, but the people in charge—the ones who had reviewed all the video of the incident—told her that no one had left any of the buildings; that everyone inside was long dead before she ever showed up.

That was when she started studying stealth tech, and she learned that everything the Empire told her about it was a lie.

They had no idea how people died inside a stealth tech field. They had never seen anything like those fading buildings before. They had no idea if the buildings existed somewhere else, if they had truly been destroyed, or if they were still standing in the same spot, a spot that the Empire never let anyone build over, just in case.

Her chest ached, just remembering those weeks after the crisis, weeks when she could barely get out of bed half the time—not that she had a bed of her own. She was staying in a government facility, which was another reason why she had avoided the dormitories here.

She started doing her own research, realized that the Empire messed with stealth tech but didn't understand it, and the scientists studying it often made it worse. She went back to school to learn everything she could about it, but when it came time to do actual experiments in stealth tech, she couldn't bring herself to do so.

She complained about the way things were, and ultimately got a black mark on her record, but it was that mark that Squishy somehow found out about. Squishy, who contacted her. Squishy, who brought her to the Nine Planets and Lost Souls to work on what was actually *anacapa* energy—which, it turned out, even the Fleet didn't completely understand, but at least they knew how to harness it, and no one ever died.

Or rarely died.

Faber wasn't really happy working in it, though, because it felt like she was playing with the materials that murdered everyone she loved.

So when Squishy came to her with the plan for destroying stealth tech in the Enterran Empire, Faber jumped at the chance. She was the first person to sign on to Squishy's so-called teams, and she became a consultant with Squishy, and she helped Squishy refine her plans as much as possible.

They agreed on one thing: they had to minimize—if not prevent—the loss of life that would come with the destruction of the backup sites.

And now, standing here, Faber realized that preventing the loss of life was the minimum she could have done. She should have prevented the loss of the other research and the destruction of these beautiful fields.

She hadn't realized that loss of beauty was almost as devastating as losing lives.

Or maybe she was just getting nervous.

"It's almost time," Bhatt said. His voice was low and gravelly. It always sounded like he hadn't spoken in weeks. An old injury, he said, but he had never told her what that injury was.

She nodded. They had calibrated their own time with the time elsewhere in the Empire. The key was to have the sites destroyed as or just before the station itself. The Empire would be dealing with its big loss long before it ever realized that the smaller ones had occurred.

Or, at least, that was the hope.

She swallowed. She had wanted to be here, to trigger the explosives and all of that destruction herself, not because she thought she would enjoy it, but because she worried that something would go wrong, and she wouldn't be close enough to fix it.

Bhatt had procured a land-and-air rover for them, one that could handle the dusty paths between the different kinds of wheat, before it would take off and fly toward the ship they'd kept hidden for months now.

Bhatt made sure no one knew he had procured the rover, and he also made sure that the ship was ready to take off.

They had to get away from all of the security monitors around the backup site before the rover flew out of here. The dust cloud from their departure would be suspicious enough; she didn't want anyone looking at the security footage—should any of it survive—long enough to figure out how she and Bhatt had escaped.

She pushed her way up the path toward the building. It was squat and a pale gold, so that it blended into the wheat fields when the stalks were high and glowed like a possible future when the fields were fallow.

Her throat tightened, and she had to figure out a way to calm herself. Maybe they would rebuild, newer, better, but just as pretty.

At least no one was inside. She had used several different measures, from heat signatures to some trackers, to make sure no one was near the site but her and Bhatt.

That had taken some planning too, but the nature of the scientific work had given her the opportunity to clear out the place. Because it had been cleared once before while she was working there.

Some of the experiments that the scientists were working on created toxic gases. And unlike work on a space station or in a starship or at a base, the environmental systems in this place weren't up to controlling the spread of the gas quickly enough to ensure the safety of everyone in the building.

The monitors worked, though, so the staff knew before the building opened for the day that it was uninhabitable. It had taken several hours to clear.

And that was the other lucky thing about the work in this facility: they had actual work hours. No one was allowed in the building over-night. It wasn't that the building was more dangerous at night or that there were established protocols that had to be followed after midnight; it was simply local custom. No one worked late unless they had some kind of security, medical, or emergency job.

Even stores and production areas were closed at night. Faber had never lived anywhere like that, and she found it decidedly odd, but it was to her benefit.

She altered the sensors so that they recorded another toxin leak, a severe one. The sensors had gone off before the site opened, and she (as well as Bhatt) had received notifications that the site was closed today.

Bhatt had set up their own monitors, to make sure no one showed up anyway and happened to be inside the building. He assured her that no one had, and the systems inside the building itself showed her that it was empty.

She pulled the manual entry card from her pocket. She was going to walk through the upper floors before destroying the place. She wanted to do a double-check.

The destruction would come in two parts: she was going to flood the upper level with the actual toxin that she had described. It was flammable. And then she would blow the lower levels, using explosives she had planted slowly during the last few weeks.

Those explosives should ignite the toxin, but if they didn't, she would manually destroy the building with some explosives she and Bhatt had in the rover.

She glanced at him. He actually looked nervous.

She didn't want the person who was supposed to guard her and protect her from all that could go wrong to look nervous.

It made her nervous.

But they had finally come to the moment they'd been preparing for.

"You ready?" she asked him.

He nodded.

Before she could change her mind, she used the manual key on the entry. One more walkthrough.

One more step before she destroyed everything.

Before she and Bhatt were able to leave.

12

QUINT PULLED OPEN THE DOOR to the communal storage area. The area sounded bigger than it was. It was barely the size of his office but littered with stealth tech tubes. They stood on shelves, on the floor, and underneath several of the tables.

The room had an odd odor, burned wires mixed with hot metal, a scent he sometimes thought of as the smell of stealth tech research. He had no idea why an area like this would accumulate that smell, particularly with the strong environmental systems that the station had, but it did, and truth be told, he didn't really like it.

Two members of the security team, bulky and scientifically illiterate, stood near the door, arms crossed. They had been keeping a wary eye on Cloris Kashion ever since she had contacted Quint.

He wanted to show her support, sure, but he also wanted everything documented, from the moment of the call until the moment he arrived.

It wasn't that he didn't trust her, exactly, it was just that she was a scientist, and Rosealma had taught him that scientists couldn't always be trusted. They lied, even to themselves.

Cloris Kashion stood in the middle of all the tubes, her auburn hair pulled away from her face. She looked worried. She was holding one of the tubes in her left hand, waving it about as if it were harmless.

The tubes weren't harmless. And they weren't really tubes. They were glass jars, filled with just enough material to start a stealth tech reaction.

When Rosealma saw this area, she went to the director of the entire station and demanded that the storage area get disassembled. *It's too dangerous,* she'd said. *You have no idea how these tubes will interact with each other.*

Quint had been there when Rosealma showed up and would have tried to stop the conversation entirely if he hadn't agreed with her, deep down. He didn't like this setup either.

He liked it even less now.

"What's the problem?" he asked Kashion.

She waggled the tube at him. "There's material in here that's not prescribed," she said.

He had no idea how she knew that. All of the materials looked unprescribed to him. A mystery, of one sort or another. Most of the materials were just strange and strangely shaped.

He even thought some of them resembled rocks—glowing, well-lit rocks, but rocks all the same.

"What kind of material?" he asked.

"I don't know," she said, "but I don't like it."

An alarm went off, distant and far away, whooping. He didn't like that either.

The security team beside him looked at him, which meant that they heard it too. Both men looked uncomfortable, as if they didn't want to be here. Or maybe they didn't want to go after the alarm.

Either way, it didn't matter. He was going to keep them here while he dealt with Kashion.

Her cheeks were flushed, and her eyes flashed. She knew something else had caught his attention. She had waited for him to arrive so she could do whatever it was she wanted to do, and now, he wasn't paying attention.

Rather than let her know that her response annoyed him, he held up a finger, indicating that she should give him a minute.

He needed to deal with that alarm first, but he knew if he left here, Kashion would do something with that tube, something that Rosealma probably wouldn't approve of.

Maybe he should bring Rosealma here, trust her in a way that would appall Beltraire, and get her to resolve this.

But that would take a lot of explanation.

Instead, he would have to deal with whatever it was that was causing the issues for Kashion. After he sent his staff to see whether that alarm was something important.

He reached his third-in-command, Anjali Pope. She had already heard the alarm and was trying to track it down. He complimented her on that, then told her to send a team to investigate before adding a few words of caution and reminding her of the necessity to respond to an alarm quickly. As if she didn't know that.

But he was doing that last bit for the record, because he'd been reprimanded in the past by management for blowing off things like smoke alarms. Usually they'd been silenced by the time he arrived because some experiment set them off.

He had a hunch, considering how that alarm warbled, that this was the case here.

But he didn't dare ignore it entirely, and he was trapped in this communal storage area with Kashion. So rather than let Pope handle all of the details, he picked the two team members who would respond. They were the kind of people who didn't get flustered by a machine reporting an error. They would take proper action and ignore the alarm if it was a malfunction.

Once that was set—and it only took about a minute or two—he let his hand drop. "Sorry," he said to Kashion, even though he wasn't sorry at all. "There was an alarm."

Kashion looked annoyed that he had put her off. Maybe she couldn't hear the alarm. Maybe it was coming through his comms and not overhead.

If that was the case, then it wasn't bad. It was something that could be dealt with quickly.

He propped the door open anyway, then took a step into the room. Kashion frowned at him. She waggled the tube again, and he wanted to hold up both hands to tell her to stop.

But, he figured, she knew more about the way that these tubes worked than he did. She knew what she could get away with and what she couldn't.

He hoped. Because that alarm wasn't shutting off, and he wanted to leave this room.

"All right," he said. "Show me."

"Three of these tubes," she said, "have tiny devices stuck to the side. They almost look like clots of dirt, but there's no dirt in here."

She held the tube upright and thrust it toward him. He was glad he wasn't close. Sometimes the materials in those tubes made his head ache.

He'd even had a woman on security who couldn't enter this communal storage area without getting a nosebleed. He'd eventually had to send her to a different location, far away from stealth tech.

Kashion twisted the tube around, then pointed at something black against the glowing rocks. "It's on three," she repeated, as if he hadn't heard her the first time.

Well, he hadn't responded to her the first time, so she could be forgiven for talking to him as if he had one-quarter the intelligence that she had. Maybe. It still irritated him.

She waggled the tube again, which just made his heart sink. That, and the continued alarm, were putting his teeth on edge.

"Explain to me why you consider that a problem," he said. He'd learned that was the best way to get scientists to talk to him like a human being, instead of the dumb guy heading security.

"These little black things," she said. "They're perfectly round. And they were evenly spaced from each other. And they're in the exact same spot on the tube. Right here."

She tapped a finger against the exterior of the tube.

The alarm was getting louder. Was there more of them? One of the security guards beside Quint clapped a hand against an ear.

There must have been something in his face—a little contempt, a bit of uncertainty?—because her expression crumpled into a massive frown.

"Oh, for the sake of…" She shook her head and grabbed at the round thing, her fingers pinched around its edges as she started to pull it off.

"No!" Quint said. "Don't—!"

A white light flared around her, one he recognized in his bones, something he still saw in his dreams. That white light had the same pearlescent gray that the light which formed around the Vallevu space station had, the moment before part of the station disappeared entirely.

Quint made that connection, grabbed the two guards, and flung them out of the door—or rather, started to fling them, when the tube Kashion was holding exploded.

The explosion pushed him backwards through that door, the guards tumbling with him. The light was moving toward the other tubes, and Quint couldn't see Kashion anymore.

His face ached, his teeth felt like they were vibrating, and that headache—that familiar headache—had formed between his brows.

He grabbed the door. It was a blast door, built to withstand the worst explosions, and he had to hope it would work now.

He needed to close it over that slow-moving white light, but he was having trouble. One of the guards picked himself off the floor. Shards of glass—or whatever those damn tubes were made of—had embedded itself into his face, but he didn't seem to notice.

The guard stumbled toward the controls by the side of the door, to see if they would close it, but Quint knew they wouldn't. The door should have shut automatically, and it hadn't.

Quint grabbed the edge of the door and pushed. The other guard joined him. Quint closed his eyes, but he could still see the white glow—and beyond it, nothing.

Nothing at all.

No wall, no Kashion, nothing.

Just like his nightmares. Just like Vallevu. Just like the disaster that destroyed him and Rosealma forever.

A voice filtered into his consciousness. It took him a moment to realize the voice was automated:

Emergency evacuation underway. Proceed to your designated evac area. If that evac area is sealed off, proceed to your secondary evac area. Do not finish your work. Do not bring your work. Once life tags move out of an area, that area will seal off. If sealed inside, no one will rescue you. Do not double back. Go directly to your designated evac area. The station will shut down entirely in...twenty...minutes.

He didn't authorize that. Which meant that Pope had to have authorized it. Which meant it had nothing to do with Kashion. Or maybe it did. Maybe the kind of explosion that had happened in this communal storage room was the kind that automatically triggered an evacuation sequence.

Normally, he would have investigated. Normally, he would have tried to see if it was warranted.

But given what he was trying to close behind this door—this blast door—this blasted door—he knew the evacuation was warranted.

The door finally moved enough for something in its frame to catch it and pull it forward. Maybe the controls had worked after all.

Quint leaned on it just long enough to catch his breath.

"An evacuation order," the guard beside him said in awe.

"Yeah," Quint said, "get the hell out of here. Don't worry about the others. Save yourself."

That was how evac orders worked. Every person for themselves. They'd all been drilled on how to get off the station in less than fifteen minutes.

Now it was time to put all of that training to the test.

All of them, except Rosealma. She had arrived after the last drill.

His heart constricted. Rosealma.

Goddammit. He still loved her. He had probably known that deep down, but now, he was sure of it.

He had to make sure she would get out of here.

He had to make sure she survived.

13

THE SHIP HAD BEEN DIFFICULT TO LAUNCH. Gorka had let Conifer do most everything, even though he was the one who, in theory, was the competent one, the one who handled all of the security and the ships and the prep. He'd lost his concentration on all of that when he let Conifer talk him into her plans.

He had thought they wouldn't need to be as careful, and he had stopped being careful.

He had made a mistake.

He finally got the ship off the moon and as far from the explosion (implosion) on Desierto Amarillo as he could without activating the FTL. He needed to get to the rendezvous site, true, but he didn't want to be early, and Conifer had made him early on everything.

Besides, he had to get rid of her body. He wasn't going to show up anywhere with a corpse in tow.

Once he got on the ship, he had gone to the medical supply closet—this runabout type ship thing was too small to have a medical bay—and got a body bag.

And then he had stopped himself.

The body bags used by the Fleet, and consequently, adopted by Lost Souls, preserved the body so that it would remain intact against the harshness of space. It was considered honorable to keep a body intact until the family had a chance to deal with it. Then the family could make its own choices.

So if he tossed her out the airlock in a body bag like he planned to do, he would have the same problem he'd had on that moon but with a twist: the Empire would identify her, and they would recognize that the body bag wasn't one of theirs. There might even be enough information inside the bag or built into the bag to let them know that it had come from Lost Souls.

He stood for a good ten minutes with his right fist clutching the body bag before he realized that he wanted the bag for his own sensibilities, not because Conifer's body needed to be wrapped in anything. She'd be a lot harder to find if she was just tossed out randomly, anyway. No beacons, no traceable materials. Just another dead soul from a ship that didn't want to keep bodies on board.

Most of those ships, though, incinerated the bodies. Either shooting them automatically with a laser weapon once they'd been launched or using some kind of body bag that would burn from the inside out.

He didn't have that kind of bag—or at least, he didn't think he did—and he didn't have the stomach to shoot a body floating away from his ship. He could probably figure out a way to make her explode, and he didn't want to do that either.

So this was how he got her to the airlock door. At least the ship had a gurney so he didn't have to carry her again, and the gurney had its own propulsion.

He knew what he was going to do: He was going to tip her off the thing into the airlock proper. Then he was going to close the interior door and open the exterior door. She would get pulled into space, and he would leave her, maybe never to be seen again.

He had to hurry because rigor mortis would start soon. He wanted to be able to fit her body into whatever space it needed to fit into, and that meant being able to bend it.

If it took three hours for rigor mortis to set in, he was getting right to the edge of that timeline now. He was racing against the strangest kind of clocks—rigor mortis, the discovery of the implosion, and the explosions all over the stealth tech backup sites five hours from the implosion Conifer had set.

Or rather, a little over two hours from now.

The area near the airlock was on a side corridor off the main corridor, one of the few design features in the entire ship. He'd had a heck of a time getting the gurney into this space, probably because this side corridor was only designed for humans to wait until their turn in the airlock.

But he managed, by tilting it just enough to get it inside. He hadn't strapped her body down because he couldn't face doing it. He had touched the body twice, and that was two times too many—the first time as he dragged her out of that base, and the second time as he maneuvered her onto the gurney.

He wasn't about to touch her again, so that meant a delicate handling of the gurney. He didn't want her sliding off too soon.

He finally had the gurney in position, and he looked at her one last time. She didn't look like the woman he had known. Her skin had gone a grayish white, and where it was cut open, the edges were flayed and curling, even paler with the lack of blood.

Her eyes were clouded over and her lips the kind of blue lips usually got when someone was too cold. She really didn't look human anymore, and he wasn't sure if that was because he had separated himself from her so much or because she had revealed herself to be without any kind of empathy at all in those last few moments of her life.

"I'm not sorry," he said to her, and knew, somehow, that simply by saying that he actually was sorry, even though he hated her.

He wasn't going to change his mind, though. He had signed onto this, and he wanted to make sure that the others would have a chance at success.

He also wanted to protect himself, and she had clearly been killed. She hadn't died accidentally. So he couldn't land anywhere without putting himself at risk.

He reached around the gurney and opened the inner airlock door. Then he tilted the gurney upright. She wasn't sliding off, though. So he pushed against the back of it. For a moment, he thought nothing happened, and then he heard a thud. The gurney tilted even farther forward.

He shoved it back into the main corridor and looked down. She hadn't even fallen right. An arm and both legs were splayed across the door.

His gorge rose. He gripped the edge of the door and used his boot to shove her body inside. She was twisted in a way that no human should ever twist. He suddenly regretted not waiting for rigor mortis, although he wasn't sure trying to squish a stiff body into the airlock would have been any better.

He had to use a lot of force to get her into that space, but he finally got all of her body parts away from the door.

Then he closed the airlock door and leaned on it for just a moment. Almost done.

He couldn't believe this day. The implosion, the fight, her death. What he had done. Who he had become. The fact that he was doing this.

He swallowed hard again, feeling vaguely nauseous. Squishy had thought everyone on the teams was stable enough to handle what they would encounter.

He had thought he was stable enough too. He had done enough for the various security and military services he'd worked for, but that was following orders. This was…different, in a way he couldn't define.

He pushed himself upright and slammed the controls with the side of his hand, opening the outer door. He didn't want to look, didn't want to see if the body got sucked out like it was supposed to.

It would be just his luck if it hadn't. But he staggered into the cockpit, and made himself look.

She was already a speck in the distance, but he recognized her as a human speck, her body still twisted slightly, legs bent oddly.

He felt a pang—no one should end up like that—and then remembered how many people she had killed without thought to any of them.

Maybe he was just as bad. Maybe. But he didn't like to think so.

And he would never discuss this with anyone, so he wouldn't know what others thought.

He would just tell Squishy and the other teams that Conifer had died when the Desierto Amarillo base imploded early. No one would ask the details, and he wouldn't offer them.

He was done with all of that.

He was done thinking about it too—or so he hoped.

14

QUINT'S FACE ACHED, but that strange headache was gone. His jaw hurt, though, and he wasn't sure if that was because he was grinding his teeth or if he had bitten down hard when that white light appeared.

The other two security guards had gone their own way, which wasn't the direction he was going. He felt like he was going the wrong way in a training competition. People ran around him, like he was a roadblock, some of them staring at him in surprise.

At first he'd thought that was because he was going in a different direction than they were and then, finally, he raised a hand to his face and winced as his fingers found a shard of that tube. He pulled the shard out, felt fresh blood moisten his skin.

He probably looked like hell. He felt like hell. And he was staggering instead of running, which probably wasn't wise.

Dozens of people were streaming past him, all of them heading toward their designated evac areas, which meant they were going in different directions, since some evac areas were on different levels and in different corridors.

He should have done more station-wide drills. He would have seen this error. Instead, he had done what the station had always done. He had assigned drills by evac vessel, timing people, so that he could figure out how long it took them to arrive from their research areas or their quarters or their offices into the proper bay, into the proper ship.

When all of them ran at once, he hadn't realized it would be such chaos. And he hadn't thought about the fact that they all were running in different directions, which had to be slowing them down.

Some were yelling at each other. A few were dragging a person with them, a person who clearly wanted to go back for something.

He heard snatches of conversation.

…hope to hell this is real. It screwed up this morning's work…

…instructions say you can't grab anything. I don't care how important…

…I'm sure she'll find her way to the vessel. You shouldn't go searching for anyone…

That last was an order embedded in the evacuation procedures, and here he was, ignoring it.

It wasn't that he thought Rosealma was too dumb to evacuate. That wasn't it at all. It was that…he didn't trust her.

He hadn't trusted her for a long time, and he was afraid she was doing something.

Plus, she had the *Dane*, and it was not her designated evac vehicle. Most people on the station weren't allowed to use their private vehicles to get out of here. It would cause too much confusion, maybe even some kind of accident in the area around the station.

The Rosealma he had known would have followed the rules. But that woman had disappeared into working against the Empire, working with the Empire's enemies, developing stealth tech.

Was the Empire so far ahead of the Nine Planets that she had come here to steal their ideas?

He hated what he was thinking. He also knew he had a good chance of being right. And he had meant to talk with her, he had, but this—this had happened before he had gotten the chance.

Before he had made the chance.

A heavyset man slammed into him, someone Quint didn't recognize, and the man nearly fell. Quint grabbed him, kept him upright, noting the sweat under the man's arms. Quint shoved him forward and then moved beyond him, wiping his own hands on his pants, noting that they were torn. He had no memory of that happening.

If Rosealma wasn't near her office, he would go to the *Dane*. He would find her, somehow, see what, exactly, was going on.

He probably should have been running toward his team, not toward his ex-wife. But he couldn't raise anyone on his comms. He was beginning to think comms were down.

But his team knew what to do. They had to be the ones to get the automated evac system going. They were probably heading toward their evac vehicles.

He should have been heading toward his.

The voice scratched overhead:

Emergency evacuation underway. Proceed to your designated evac area. If that evac area is sealed off, proceed to your secondary evac area. Do not finish your work. Do not bring your work. Once life tags move out of an area, that area will seal off. If sealed inside, no one will rescue you. Do not double back. Go directly to your designated evac area. The station will shut down entirely in...fifteen...minutes.

He had no idea where the past five minutes went, but they had vanished. And he had to get to Rosealma.

He rounded a corner, and there she was. Her short hair was perfect, her clothing pristine. She was yelling at people, pushing them, really, trying to get them out of the corridor and toward their evac areas.

She looked like she was in charge of security for this station, not him.

A jar stood at her feet. It pulsed. The jar looked like it might contain stealth tech material. She didn't even seem to be aware of it.

He wanted to run to her and grab it, fling it far away so that it wouldn't turn white and obliterate the entire corridor.

Obliterate her.

The corridor was clearing. The first mass dash of scientists and others was subsiding. He couldn't even hear steps in the corridor any longer.

He ran toward her—only it didn't quite feel like running. It felt painful, as if there was extra gravity in every movement he made.

He reached her side, and she flinched. What was on his face, his expression, his reaction that made her flinch?

Was Rosealma afraid of him? That made no sense. He had never hurt her.

But they had hurt each other emotionally those last few years. They had nearly destroyed each other.

He grabbed her free arm, maybe a tad too tightly. There was anger underneath his movements, and he tried to set that aside.

He blamed her for this. He realized it the moment he touched her.

"We have to evacuate," he said, and realized how dumb that sounded. She knew that, but she was staying behind for a reason. He just wasn't sure what that reason was.

"I'm going to go," she said. "I want to make sure everyone's out."

That wasn't her responsibility. That was the responsibility of his people and he trusted them to handle it, even though he couldn't reach them.

"They're out," he said of the scientists and the engineers and everyone in the station. He didn't know they were out for certain, but he had seen enough to know they would be. They had gone through the drills. They knew how to make it to their evac areas, and they knew how important that was.

He pulled her, loosening his grip just a little.

"Let's go," he said. He wanted her beside him. He needed her to get out of here, now.

She shook her head. Her gaze was moving past him, scanning the corridor. But no one had run past them the entire time they'd been talking.

If there were still people to evacuate, they would be coming by right now. They knew that they only had a short window to escape, and they had always taken that seriously.

"You go," she said. "I'll catch up."

He wanted to shake her, and realized the anger he was feeling right now wasn't just for this moment. It was for their entire time together.

Maybe Beltraire had been right: maybe there was a lot more behind Quint's interaction with Rosealma than he realized.

His fingers loosened on her arm. "Rosealma," he said tiredly, "we're not doing this again."

Her gaze hit him, and it was cold. "Yes, we are," she said. "Get out *now*."

"I'm not leaving you," he said.

Her jaw set, and he knew in that moment he had lost the argument, at least this way.

"Get out, Quint," she said through clenched teeth. "I can take care of myself."

He knew that phrase. She had used it so many times with him, and he had never heard it as a warning, but it always was. He had learned that.

Maybe if he tried a different tactic.

"Rosealma, I'm sorry—"

"Oh, for God's sake," she said. "Get *out*."

And then she shoved him away from her. He staggered backwards, and nearly fell, catching himself at the very last second, his heart pounding in his chest.

Apparently, he wasn't the only one with leftover anger from the marriage.

Which meant that they could stay in this corridor and fight until the entire station blew—or whatever was going to happen—or he could let her follow her plan.

He straightened his feet, trying to stand upright, and his heel caught that jar. It clattered over, and he stared at it, praying it wouldn't explode.

"Do we need that?" he asked. Was it what she had been trying to use/save/do while she was here?

"Aren't you listening?" she said. "You're supposed to leave everything behind."

"You didn't make the rules," he snapped, and regretted the words immediately, because that anger he'd been trying to control, the one that reflected in her face, had come out through his voice.

"Those aren't my rules," she said. "They're the station's."

And she didn't sound too happy with that. He wondered if she wanted him gone so she could pick up that jar and carry it out of here.

"Now, hurry." Her tone had softened. Apparently, she also realized that the anger wasn't doing either of them any good. "I'll be right behind you."

He hoped she wasn't lying to him. She'd lied to him in the past, before she became the new Rosealma, and he always fell for it.

If she was lying now, it might kill her.

"Promise me you won't do anything stupid, Rosealma," he said.

She half-smiled at him. "When have I ever done anything stupid?"

If only he had time to answer that. He could feel the pull of the argument. It would be so easy to continue, to fight with her until whatever happened happened.

"Rosealma," he said, without even realizing he had been about to say it.

Her voice was very soft now, and warm. "*Go*," she said quietly.

He didn't want to leave her, but weirdly, he knew that was the only way to get her off the station.

He whirled, oriented himself, then half-ran half-walked away from her.

He wasn't going to his designated evac area either.

He would wait for her. On the *Dane*.

15

THE BOAT BOBBLED IN THE WATER, and Etheni felt her own stomach bobble with it. In her right hand, she clutched the remote detonator. The wind had started up and it was playing with her hair. The sky overhead was a grayish white, which she had come to recognize as the beginnings of a stormy afternoon.

Which was not what she needed. She had enough trouble with boats. If she had known that her stomach was one of those that moved with the waves, she would have asked to destroy a different backup site.

Cleta was inside the pilot house, the highest point on the boat. The spray from the waves had coated the windows, and she could barely see him in there. He was scanning their equipment to make sure they weren't being followed.

But there was no reason to follow them. No one suspected them of anything. They hadn't *done* anything yet.

Her mouth was dry. A wave hit the side of the boat, spray foaming over the edge, some of it hitting her cheeks. Cold. The Seltaana sea water was always cold, which she had learned shortly after arriving here. She'd wanted to swim in it, and everyone had discouraged her, saying that there were riptides, and the water itself was cold enough to kill her.

She wiped at her face with the back of her left hand. The island was receding. If she wasn't careful, the boat would be out of range of the remote detonator.

She glanced at the pilot house. Cleta had moved closer to her, almost as though he was going to come down the two stairs toward the deck, to encourage her to set off the detonator as soon as possible.

She didn't need encouragement. She was watching the time. She knew that she had to set off the detonator.

But part of her was waiting for the three people still in the backup station to leave. And they weren't.

Of course they weren't. Their shift wasn't done yet.

More spray hit her face, drenching her.

She could barely see the building through the growing mist. The wind was getting fierce, and her hair was whipping into her face.

She had thought she was more decisive than this. More courageous. More determined.

Cleta waved a hand from the pilot house, but then disappeared into its depths. Only a moment later, she understood why.

The boat was not bobbing any longer. It was actually diving up and down on the waves.

She took a deep breath, got a taste of salt and brine and wet. It tasted like sadness.

It tasted like defeat.

She and Cleta could go to the meet-up and she could tell Squishy, *I'm sorry. I couldn't get three people out of the backup station*, and Squishy would—what? Get mad? Wonder if she had tried hard enough? Understand?

Etheni's stomach twisted. She couldn't tell Squishy that. She couldn't look Squishy in the eye and tell her that the only reason stealth tech as practiced by the Empire still existed was because Etheni had lost her nerve.

She raised her hand very slowly, her right hand with the remote detonator.

Technically, she could have been inside the pilot house with Cleta, but she wasn't. She didn't trust the detonator to work in there, even though she knew that there didn't have to be line of sight. The detonator worked beneath piles of steel. It would activate the devices she placed underneath the building, interacting with all of the equipment, and start a chain reaction in each drawer, reactions that would build one on another, until the energy of all of those reactions destroyed the drawers, the backups, the remote contact ports, the floor, the walls, and the building itself.

There was movement from the pilot house again. Cleta coming toward her.

Her cheeks burned. If she didn't do this, she would fail, not just Cleta and Squishy and everyone else on the various teams. She would fail herself.

She squeezed her hand around the remote, pulled it closer, and then pressed the combination that would set it off. The combination was complex, only because she didn't want anyone to accidentally set it off.

Cleta reached her side just as the remote turned green.

"Done?" he asked.

She didn't have to answer him. There was a whomp so loud that the force of the sound knocked them both back.

He swore and ran for the pilot house. If there was that kind of blowback just from the sound, then there would be consequences from the explosion itself.

He made it into the pilot house almost before Etheni realized she needed to move. She sprinted after him, her feet slipping on the wet deck.

The water was swirling, the air no longer smelled like salt and fish, but like burning metal.

Her eyes burned. A cloud had formed over the island. The cloud was black and gray and a weird kind of orange.

It took her a moment to realize the orange came from something burning.

She took one last glance at the island. The middle looked like it had fallen into the sea.

Nothing could survive that.

No one could survive that.

She let out a shaky breath, and climbed the two steps into the pilot house, pulling the door closed.

"Hang on," Cleta said. "This is going to be a bumpy ride."

She didn't care.

She sank into the chair next to his and bowed her head, her back to the island now. But debris—black and gray and still glowing red—was raining around them.

She hoped she wouldn't see bodies. She could barely handle this.

She wasn't sure she could handle bodies.

She wasn't sure she could handle anything anymore.

But then, she didn't need to.

Her part in this was done.

Escape was up to Cleta now.

16

BELTRAIRE CAME OUT OF FTL sooner than he expected. He had gotten an urgent notification. Urgent notifications used some technology he didn't understand so that ships traveling faster than the speed of light got an important message.

Second backup station gone. Location, Seltaana Sea...

And the rest got garbled. So he had to come out of FTL immediately, his stomach churning. He hadn't been heading to that site. He'd been heading to the Zargasa site to see what information he could glean.

By coming out of FTL here, he was far short of Zargasa. He would have to return to FTL to get there.

He ran a hand through his hair, then made himself focus.

He'd known that implosion at Desierto Amarillo was intentional because the satellites had been destroyed, but he hadn't known how it happened. But he had assumed that the saboteurs were heading to the other sites.

He had thought coordination would be possible, but he had been hoping that wasn't how this had been planned.

Although the equipment failures at Zargasa had argued for coordination rather than a moving band of saboteurs.

But now, with the loss of the station on the Seltaana Sea, he wasn't sure what to think.

He kept the ship moving forward as he checked his feeds.

The Seltaana Sea station didn't implode—not right away. There was a series of tiny explosions, and then a big explosion, that made the entire building collapse.

At least three lives lost.

The entire island was now enveloped in a cloud of smoke and debris and ash.

He could actually reprogram his flight path and go there. His ship was equidistant from the Desierto Amarillo station and the Seltaana Sea station.

But neither of them needed him right now. He wasn't even sure if going to Zargasa was the right move. That was an old station. Maybe the equipment failures were simply coincidence.

There had been no equipment failures reported from the Desierto Amarillo station or the Seltaana Sea station before they blew. And they both imploded, although it didn't look like the Seltaana Sea destruction had been triggered from orbit.

He let out a breath.

He needed to figure out which of the other backup stations was going to blow next. Or if they all were. Or if he could get close to one and stop it from being destroyed.

Damn Quint for sending him out here alone.

Beltraire needed to stay out of FTL for the next few minutes. He needed to send more than a casual alert to the other stations.

He needed to have them actively search for a saboteur.

He needed to stop this all—right now.

17

THE ELEVATOR TOOK KOH to the main level of Zargasa Station. She wiped the back of her arm over her face, then wished she hadn't. Her skin came away gray, like that dust.

It was probably in her lungs. She knew it was in her nostrils, her eyes, and it coated her lips. She wanted to wipe them off and she wasn't quite sure how.

The elevator opened into the physical plant. It had taken Noor nearly three weeks to get the codes which allowed her into the physical plant. If Noor had the educational background, he could have done the work himself. It would have been easy for him to be in here—working as he did for security—and it was odd for her to be here.

Not to mention that she was leaving actual footprints. That dust from the backup level covered every inch of her, which she hadn't expected.

She kept trying to tell herself that it was all right; that the dust would simply make the equipment on this level malfunction quicker, but the dust—and her footprints—looked like a confession.

She had gone slightly crazy down there, in her claustrophobic state. She had scurried from floor to floor, not paying as close attention as she should have when she placed the devices. She had been working from the bottom of the facility to the top, which she had initially thought caused her claustrophobia, but she had to wonder. Maybe she'd had it all along and hadn't realized it.

Because the elevator had unnerved her as well.

The physical plant held the controls for a wide variety of things, from the environmental system inside the entire station to the mechanical room that housed the equipment to the supply cabinet that held all of the tools for fixing things.

There were many ways to tamper with everything in here, which was why this area was locked off and considered the most secure part of a scientific research station. But it wasn't secure enough, since she got in here.

The dust didn't coat everything in this room. It looked relatively clean, albeit old. The equipment seemed like it had come from a deep dark time in human history, with its gears and cranks and wheezing fans.

This was the oldest of the backup sites, a repurposed station that had once housed—she had no idea what it had housed. But something old and important to the Empire.

She had gotten used to the way things were at Lost Souls, with the new equipment and the clean lines of Fleet technology. Here, in the Empire, people were allowed to assemble equipment out of whatever they found. The Empire actually took pride in repurposing things it had found or things that had been abandoned or left behind.

And the standards—they were so low as to be nonexistent, at least in her mind. The columns and posts below, where she had set the explosives, were different sizes and different shapes. Some were made of a metal that was clearly rusting, which just appalled her.

The weight of the building (and the mountain?) might come down on everything even without her help.

But what might have happened no longer mattered. What would happen—and soon—was what mattered.

She was sweating. It was warmer in here than she liked. The equipment actually gave off heat, which told her that it had probably been poorly manufactured.

A bead of sweat ran along the side of her face and dripped onto her shirt, leaving a light grayish brown stain. When she got out of here, she would take the longest shower of her life.

Noor could pilot the ship and get them to the rendezvous point. She would shower, and shower, and shower.

Provided she got this done.

She wiped the damp palms of her hand against her pants and walked to the environmental system. There were, according to Noor, only twenty people in the building. She could get them out with one act of sabotage.

She poked open the environmental system door. It banged against the wall, and she let out a small sigh of relief. The controls on the environmental system looked just like they were supposed to.

She had been worried, given what she had seen down below, that nothing would look familiar.

She flicked off everything—air, lights, temperature controls. Immediately, the room around her went black—so dark she couldn't even see her hands in front of her face.

The environmental controls were powered by a tiny internal generator, though, so they remained on and blinking.

Not that it mattered. She pulled a glove she had taken from one of the space suits from her pocket and slipped it onto her left hand. Then she turned the knuckle lights on low, just so she could see what she was doing, not so that she would blind herself with some kind of reflection.

Then she removed a small laser from her pocket. She held the laser steadily in her right hand and carefully burned the controls, making it impossible to repair what she had done.

The air smelled of fried equipment and hot metal, and the smell didn't dissipate the way that it would have if the air were moving. It was stuffy in here now, and getting hotter, and she hated it, almost as much as being in those tunnels underneath this building.

She moved to the backup equipment, which was separate for each system—lighting, temperature, and air quality. She shut off those systems too, even though they hadn't kicked on (shouldn't they have kicked on?) and burned their controls as well.

Her heart rate had slowed just enough to make her calmer. Getting the work done eased her mind.

She smiled to herself, then pocketed the laser. She had one last thing to do: she turned to the security system and pushed a fire alarm button for a room deep inside the mountain. Fire suppression systems immediately came on, along with the alarms, ordering an immediate evacuation.

The scientists—well, everyone who worked in the station—was taught to evacuate first, solve problems later. They weren't allowed to bring their research or grab their personal items. They had to flee.

She used the knuckle lights to illuminate the path ahead of her. The light was a pale white against equipment she couldn't quite name. She wound her way around the floor, got to the main door, and opened it slowly, half expecting someone to disobey standing orders and come here to see what was going on.

But the exterior corridor was empty. No one was even running past her.

Maybe Noor had gotten most everyone to leave before the fire alarm went off. That had been the plan after all.

She smiled grimly to herself. She felt calmer now, and she couldn't tell if that was because the job was nearly done or if it was because she no longer had a sense that she was underneath the mountain.

Not that it mattered. She pulled the door closed behind her, and heard the lock click into place.

Then she ran, just like she was supposed to, for the nearest exit.

18

QUINT'S DESIGNATED EVAC AREA was all the way across the station, on one of the private docking bays set aside for staff. Even if he wanted to run to that bay, he wouldn't make it in time.

The last time the androgynous voice had informed him of how many minutes were left before the station blew, the time was eleven minutes. And he knew, better than anyone, that these projections could sometimes be very, very wrong.

He headed for the bay with the *Dane* inside, constantly checking over his shoulder for Rosealma. But she hadn't followed him.

His heart pounded. She was going to leave. She had to leave. She wasn't suicidal. He would have known.

Still, just outside the bay doors, he opened one of the environmental controls and looked for heat signatures. Besides his, there was only one. Rosealma's. And it had started to move.

He wiped his heat signature from the system, so she couldn't find him. He hoped it would also shut down the overhead voice, but the second he had that thought, the voice began again:

Emergency evacuation underway. Proceed to your designated evac area....

He didn't pay attention to the rest. Instead, he dragged himself into the docking bay. The injuries he had sustained when that tube exploded (when Kashion died) were exhausting him. Either he had been infected with some of that bad energy or he was losing more blood than he realized.

But he set that aside. He had to. He needed to get to the *Dane*.

The docking bay doors opened, and he let out a gasp of surprise. The nearest ships were already gone. He'd never seen this bay so empty.

The *Dane* was to his right. It wasn't a single ship and it wasn't an orbiter, not at least the kind of orbiter that he was familiar with. It looked like one of the ships that had come into the Empire from the Nine Planets, usually searching for some kind of trade or work for the person inside.

He'd vetted the *Dane* when it had first arrived, but he had never found its provenance. He did know who named it though. Rosealma had clearly changed its designation, because the ship was named for Erasmus Dane, one of their old professors—someone they had bonded over.

Dane had hated Rosealma because she had dared contradict him, and she had been right to do so. Quint hadn't been certain of that at the time, but he was now.

As he approached the *Dane*, it shuddered. He'd never seen it do that. Then he realized what had to be happening: Rosealma was using some kind of remote starter.

That made his life much easier. He didn't have to let himself into the ship and then explain to Rosealma that he'd been breaking in all along to check up on her.

Instead, she had just guaranteed that he could get in without raising any questions at all.

As if in answer to that thought, the exit on the side closest to him eased open, and a ramp deployed. He glanced at the bay doors, saw that they were still closed, and limped toward the ramp.

He wasn't dripping blood, so he was doing better than he had thought he would be. He wouldn't be leaving a trail, so she wouldn't expect him to be inside.

He gripped the handrail that was built onto the ramp and pulled himself up. He didn't like the depth of the exhaustion he felt. It wasn't natural.

But he managed to get inside and let out a small breath.

The cruiser—if that's what this could be called—was small by most standards. It had a cockpit that expanded into an eating area and seating, if this thing had more than two passengers. The galley kitchen divided the cockpit from the other room, which had a pulldown bed and lots of storage.

He'd already familiarized himself with everything in this place over the past several months, as he tried to figure out what Rosealma was up to.

The ship was vibrating slightly because its engine was on. All of the startup procedures were underway, which relieved him more than he could say.

There had been a small part of him—or maybe a not-so-small part of him—that had been afraid that the Rosealma he had always known was completely gone. That this woman, as much as she looked like his Rose, would actually let herself die when the station exploded.

But she was his Rose. She wasn't going to die, unless her death was accidental. She was going to arrive at this ship soon enough.

The last thing he wanted was a confrontation with her. They'd already proven in that corridor that they could lose track of time arguing, and they didn't have time to lose.

He slipped into the second room. The bed was still pulled up into the wall, only the faint outline showing where it could be. There were two circles on the floor, marking the spot where chairs could rise up if someone wanted them.

He ran a hand against the edge of that bed, feeling the tracers he had put there the very first time he had explored this ship. He'd been on the *Dane* several times since Rosealma had arrived on the station. First, he'd gone through her network, hoping to learn more than he already knew. Then he'd planted tracers, in case she left suddenly.

He wanted to be able to track her. He'd never expected to hide on this ship, while he was waiting for her, while he was hoping she would arrive in time.

He leaned against the wall, thankful for the support against his back.

At the moment, all the room held were two closets full of clothing and small boxes of tokens and trinkets, things he had looked at before. None of them meant anything to him, but they meant something to Rosealma.

He'd have to ask her what they were, maybe, once the ship was underway.

Something chirruped. He closed the door to the room most of the way, leaving only a crack in the center.

The ship shook very hard, and footsteps pounded. Rosealma burst through the same entrance that he had used, slamming a hand on the control panel so that the door shut.

Then she launched herself at the seat in the cockpit, moving faster than he had ever seen her move. She was breathing hard—clearly, she had run here.

If his sense of time was right, they only had minutes to spare to get out of here. The crack in the door gave him just enough of a view of the cockpit that he could see her, hands moving rapidly as she set everything in place.

She didn't pull up any screens, though, and she didn't open the cockpit windows either. She was going to pilot her way out of here using instruments—or maybe let the ship itself do it.

He hoped she wouldn't let the ship do it.

But he had no say in this. If he let her know he was here right now, there was a chance—not a good chance, but a chance—that she would toss him off the ship.

And maybe his designated evac vehicle remained in the private bay or maybe it didn't. He had no idea.

What he did know was that he probably didn't have the time to get there, even if he was being optimistic.

The *Dane*'s vibration eased, the sign of any well-made ship rising off a floor and getting ready to fly away. He moved away from the door. He didn't want to lose his footing and alert her to his presence.

Instead, he went to the far corner of the room and sank onto the floor. He leaned his head back, feeling the stinging ache in his skin.

He closed his eyes and hoped she would get them out of there before the entire station blew up.

19

THEY HAD BARELY MADE IT OFF the landing platform and over the valley when the mountaintop blew.

Gagne clutched the controls on the ship, feeling them wobble beneath her. She'd been so concerned with Skopf's frostbite that she hadn't thought to activate the shields on the ship. She'd believed she had more time.

She hadn't realized the mountaintop would blow so quickly.

Debris rose straight up and sideways, with a force she hadn't expected. She had to steer around several boulder-sized bits of mountain as she made her way toward orbit.

Fortunately, the ship was as gray as the rocks, so that nothing—no tracking device, no camera, nothing—would show the ship as anything other than some debris.

She hoped.

If the cameras survived.

If any equipment survived at all.

She was flying into the middle of that ice storm, but it had no effect on the ship. Once she and Skopf had gotten inside the ship, they were safe.

But Skopf didn't look safe. His face was red in places, and a strange, scarred white in others. It was the white that the handheld medical device she had given him seemed to want to concentrate on.

She would have helped him, but now she was focused on escape—not from Destination Heights itself, but from the debris she had caused in the explosion.

"That happened faster than I thought," Skopf said—or rather, mumbled. He was having trouble moving his lips. Hell, he was having trouble moving his entire face.

"Yeah," she said without looking at him. If she looked at him, he would know that what she was about to say next was a lie. "It happened faster than I thought too."

She hadn't told him that she had added a few more explosives at the last minute. She had wanted everything to end as quickly as possible.

Something scraped the side of the ship, and she had to focus on flying again. Most of the debris was heading downward now, after the initial force of the explosion.

She couldn't help herself. She had to fly over the mountaintop to see what, exactly, she had done.

She turned and dove back through the clouds. It took a moment to realize that she *was* through the clouds. What she had thought was clouds was actually fine dust from the mountaintop. Dust and clumps of snow, blown skyward and caught in the still strong prevailing winds.

She wasn't sure she would be able to see the mountaintop—or what was left of it, and then she found an area where the debris thinned.

The mountain was suddenly visible, and the top, well, it was in a completely different place.

When she and Skopf landed here months ago, the mountaintop was a literal peak, snow-covered and sharp, the base built into the side like an icicle that had formed on the side of a building.

But now, the mountaintop wasn't really a top. It was more like the shell of a mountain, with a bowl in the middle. And inside that bowl, she could see flames licking skyward.

There was nothing left of that base, nothing left of the peak either. Much of the debris was rolling down the mountain's sides, some of it taking trees along with it. The destruction was continuing, even though the blast was over.

Skopf mumbled something. She turned to see him standing beside her, hand resting on what normally would have been the back of his own chair. He was swaying slightly.

"We have to go," he said—or sort of said. It was easier for her to understand him when she faced him and saw him attempt to form words.

She nodded, flew out of the debris cloud and then headed to orbit.

She wasn't going to set the coordinates for the rendezvous point yet, on the off chance that they got caught. She would feel better when they were far from this place.

She would feel better when they were out of the Empire altogether.

20

Beltraire was sending out the second of his carefully worded emergency alerts when he saw yet another flare on one of his screens. He enlarged the image and saw the mountaintop on Telaan blow, and the backup site that some idiot had named Decision Heights for the mountain itself obliterated in a haze of dust and debris.

He let out a breath and cursed. He hadn't sent a warning there yet. He was trying to walk a balance between telling the local authorities that the Empire had a secret protected site on Telaan and emphasizing how important it was to guard that site.

And he'd been too late.

He'd just sent notice to Wuhtmu, letting them know that someone would probably try to breach their space, and then backed it up with a notification to the local authorities in the tiny town of Olita where a lot of the base workers lived.

He'd been as circumspect as possible, and now he wished he hadn't. This hadn't been the time for crafting a carefully worded warning. He should have told them directly that saboteurs were on the loose, and that he would answer pertinent questions later.

At least he had let the sites know they needed to backup their information as quickly as possible. He had sent that message hours ago, and with luck, someone somewhere had followed his orders.

He wiped a hand over his face and thought of telling Quint. But right now, he was too pissed at Quint to send him a message. Quint could figure this out on his own.

Beltraire now knew where he was headed. He was going to Wuhtmu. If he used his stardrive, he would get there shortly, and maybe even catch one of the saboteurs.

He needed to find out who they were, and who they worked for.

He needed answers, and he figured the only way to get them was to look for them himself.

21

THE RESEARCH BUILDING WAS CLEAR. Faber had double-checked it and fought the urge to triple-check it.

Instead, she went outside and immediately got overwhelmed by the dry, sharp scent of wheat. She locked the exit, even though she didn't have to, and stuffed the manual key in her pocket.

Then she backed away from the building, nearly backing into Bhatt. He had a hand shaded over his face.

The air was getting hot, and the sun was intense. The humidity made little heat waves above the swaying wheat.

She took one of the remotes from him. She had to do the top part first because it would take a good five minutes to flood the entire upper levels of that building with toxic gas.

"You need to get back," she said to him.

"You too," he said.

She nodded. She wanted to stay close, to see if everything worked, but he had a tablet that would monitor everything. It didn't matter if more alarms went off, because everyone in Olita thought the toxic gas already flooded the entire building.

With her right thumb, she pressed the button releasing the gas. Such a simple movement. Something that seemed so deceptively easy, not counting all the planning and work she had done.

She backed away, then grabbed Bhatt's arm, about to pull him toward the place where they had hidden the rover. But he put a hand over hers, stalling them.

For a moment, her heart rate spiked, and she tried to pretend the hesitation wasn't making her panic.

She didn't want to go back inside. She didn't want to set anything manually. She had mentally said goodbye to this place, the wheat and all the people she had known here.

Then he looked sideways at her.

"It's done," he said. "We need to get out of here."

She nodded, took her hand off his arm, and put her palm against the small of his back, propelling him forward. He started to run, and she followed. The rover wasn't far from here, but it was far enough.

She needed to be inside the rover, and it had to be moving before she triggered the explosive devices. She had no idea how long it would take to ignite the gas inside, but she had a hunch it would be seconds instead of minutes.

The last few steps. She was nearly out of here.

The mission would be over.

And her revenge would be complete.

22

THE *DANE* RUMBLED AND THEN CATAPULTED FORWARD so hard that Quint rocked back and forth against the wall. If he hadn't had his arms around his head, he would have hit it, hard, against the corner he was sitting in.

Then the *Dane* stabilized and it felt as comfortable inside the ship as it had on the station.

And it shouldn't have. The *Dane* should have gone into FTL right away, and that transition was always rockier than the one from a standing start into a normal speed.

Was Rosealma having trouble with the ship? That would be just their luck. He would have come on board to get away from the station and to quiz Rosealma, and instead, he would die with her.

He pushed himself up, wiped his hands on his tattered clothing, and wished, suddenly, he'd been able to bring something else.

Beltraire would have laughed at him—more proof that Quint was still in love with Rosealma—and Quint mentally had to give him that. Quint would never lose the attraction to her, and he would never lose his fascination with her.

Ever.

He just had to work around it now.

Because that evacuation of the station wasn't a coincidence.

Maybe she had figured out how to get everyone off the station so that her own people could come in and—

And do what, exactly? Steal the research? She probably could have done that on her own. And he'd seen some reports that led him to believe that whatever Rosealma had been doing for the Nine Planets was much more sophisticated than what the Empire was doing, at least when it came to stealth tech research.

He walked to the door, a bit gingerly, because his muscles were sore and he ached everywhere. He still had no idea what that explosion—or whatever it was called—had done to him, not exactly. He wondered if Rosealma would know.

He opened the door ever so quietly, so she wouldn't hear him at all, and emerged into the cockpit.

Rosealma was sitting in the pilot's chair, staring at screens all around her. He could see what was on the screens too. The station, receding in the distance, but not fast enough.

Rosealma's right hand hovered over some controls and her fingers were shaking ever so slightly.

Was she waiting for someone to appear? The ships he feared she had called, maybe? Someone coming to take over the station and maybe use it as a base to attack the Empire, a place to launch ships from or maybe create new weapons, or maybe even something else he hadn't thought of, not yet.

He leaned against the wall, crossed his arms, and was about to speak when a white glow started in the middle of the station.

He glanced at another screen and saw the same thing. Then at a third, and saw that the white glow was growing.

His stomach twisted. That white was the same color as the white that had engulfed Kashion.

So much for his theories. The station was going to explode.

Rosealma slammed her palm against the FTL controls—probably too late. He let out a breath, wondering for the third time this day if he was going to die.

Her shaking hand touched four parts of the control board. Rosealma was leaning forward, cursing, and then the screens went dark.

The ship shuddered, as he had expected it to do a few minutes ago, and he pushed his back against the wall so that he wouldn't lose his balance.

The screens were dark, the station was gone, and then Rosealma collapsed forward in her chair, hiding her face in her hands.

Had she expected that implosion—explosion—whatever happened back there?

Whatever happened was clear on one level, though. The evacuation order had been the right thing: the station was gone.

Her shoulders were shaking too, and he longed to walk up to her, slip his arms around her, and comfort her.

But that wouldn't have worked in the best of times, and this was not the best of times.

Besides, he had some decisions to make. He needed to find out how culpable she was in that destruction.

He shifted, not trying to be quiet any longer, but she didn't seem to hear him.

So he said, "You want to explain to me what the fuck just happened?"

She jumped. He'd never seen her do that. She whirled in her seat, her face pale. She had assumed she was alone; he could see it in her eyes.

His presence both surprised and startled her.

She dropped her hands slowly, and took a deep, slow breath. Some things about Rosealma never changed. She always moved slowly when she was trying to hide profound emotions.

She turned her chair toward him. Then her gaze took all of him in, starting at his face and working its way down to his boots. It took a moment for her to meet his eyes again.

She hadn't answered him in any meaningful way. So he raised his eyebrows, effectively asking his question again.

You want to explain to me what the fuck just happened?

"The station blew up," she said. "Or it was blowing up, just like we knew it would."

His mind caught the wording, wondered if she meant "we" as in him and her, and the fact that they knew came from the evacuation announcement, or if the "we" meant her and her team, whoever that might be, and they knew the station would blow because they planted explosives.

He would bet on the second, because of the tiny device that had engulfed Kashion.

"I just hit the FTL," Rose was saying. She was almost babbling—or rather, doing the thing that was the closest to babbling that she did. She talked sometimes when she shouldn't.

He had learned long ago that if he remained silent, she might reveal more than she realized.

"The last thing we want," she said in her most reasonable tone, "is to be near that part of space. There's a good chance that explosion could open an interdimensional rift."

That surprised him. He had no idea what that even meant.

"A what?" he asked, unable to keep silent any longer.

"An interdimensional rift."

He hated it when she repeated the same words. It was the concept he didn't understand, not the words.

And maybe remembering those arguments from the past, she added, "The stealth tech was unstable."

That was not an explanation. That was *never* an explanation. She was treating him as if he was an idiot.

"Stealth tech has always been unstable," he snapped, and in those words—or, rather, in that tone—he recognized the same frustration he had always felt around her. "You know that better than most."

They were easing into the old pattern, fighting again when it was better to work together. But he couldn't seem to stop himself.

Or maybe he was just angry at her for deflecting. Because she really didn't answer his question about the interdimensional rift, and there was something in her tone…

She raised her chin, her eyes hooded. Her hands were still shaking.

"Yes," she said. "*Stealth tech* has always been unstable."

The emphasis intrigued him. Stealth tech as opposed to what?

"But this time," she continued, "the entire research station paid the price instead of a few volunteers."

Her words took his breath away. "A few...?" She knew better than that. She knew exactly how many had died in the past.

She had always thrown that in his face.

"Only this time," she added, "no one died."

She sounded proud. Any doubt he'd had before about her ties to this destruction faded when she uttered those words.

No one died. Kashion had died. And decades of research—centuries, maybe—was gone.

Unless Beltraire saved the other backup sites.

Anger flashed through Quint. He tamped it down, though. He let her think that he was not onto her.

He would find out what she had done. He would figure out why.

And what to do next.

23

THE RENDEZVOUS SITE WAS AN ABANDONED SPACE STATION as far from the border between the Empire and the Nine Planets as possible. If anything, the rendezvous site was too deep into Empire space to be safe, but Squishy had said—at that last meeting—that the rendezvous had to be far away from the Nine Planets—and Lost Souls—so that no one would track them there.

Her theory was that if the group ended up too close to the Nine Planets and the Empire somehow connected them all to the explosions, then the Empire would attack the Nine Planets—and maybe destroy them.

She didn't want to be the cause of that.

Gorka had always thought that the choice of the station was disingenuous. He had even argued that, more than once, and got Squishy's patented withering look. She hadn't thought much of him, and she had probably been right.

But then again, she had trusted Conifer, and see where that had gotten them? It had brought a lot more deaths than Squishy had ever wanted.

The space station had been Empire built and Empire-run, but it had been partially destroyed in an explosion more than 100 years ago. Squishy had, in theory, done research on that explosion, and she had said it wasn't stealth tech or anything research based.

It had been a good, old-fashioned accident, a ship losing control as it tried to hit the docking ring and plowing through one entire level of the station, nearly slicing it in half.

The extent of the disaster had led to an abandonment of the station, all under the pretense that the station would be repaired at one point.

But its useful life had nearly been over when it got hit. The regular space routes had moved far away from the station, and it wasn't near an inhabited planet. Maintaining it cost a lot of money, and fixing it would cost more, so the Empire took the opportunity provided by the accident and abandoned the station.

They'd cleaned out much of it, but the general shape of it was still intact. There were still interior apartments and the spaces set aside for bars and restaurants. There were separate areas for officials, and there was a secondary docking ring, which was where they were all supposed to land.

Then the teams were supposed to meet inside the station, in what had been a bar overlooking the docking ring.

But it was all empty and cold and dark—everything about the station. He'd circled it twice in his little ship, expecting someone else to be here.

No one else was.

The fact that he was alone made him shake. The events of the past several hours had finally caught up to him. If he closed his eyes, he saw Conifer's body, floating away from him—or, more accurately, remaining stationary while he traveled away from it.

He didn't want to be the only one who survived. He didn't want to sit at this rendezvous point for the required twenty-four hours, waiting and waiting and waiting for people who would never arrive.

He wasn't sure he could handle any of this—all of this—on his own.

His breath hitched, and he actually felt tears. Then he straightened his back and made himself breathe.

He had no time for self-pity. He'd learned that long ago, when he'd learned how to defend entire starships. Events could either break you or build you, and all of his life, he'd chosen to be formed by the events around him, rather than let them break him.

He didn't dare focus on what had happened this morning—the deaths, the confrontation with Conifer, her death. He had to set those aside, pretend they hadn't happened.

And, as he had learned so long ago, sometimes when you pretended something hadn't happened, you could bury it in the recesses of your mind, never to be seen again.

He knew such a plan was dangerous—sometimes old memories surfaced from that storage box at the most inconvenient times—but he had no other choice.

He could melt down in this ship, alone with his newly formed memories, or he could follow instructions and wait here for twenty-four hours.

Then he checked the ship's clock against the timetable that Squishy had set, and was stunned to see that he was still early.

He had arrived here just as the other backup sites were being destroyed. And then the station itself would get destroyed.

He didn't have twenty-four hours to wait. He had thirty.

He let out a small breath. Figuring out that he had arrived here before everyone else, even given what had happened, eased his mind considerably.

Yes, he would be alone with his thoughts for several hours, but he already had been.

And he could make use of the time by seeing if he could figure out how to seal off the section of the station where the teams would meet, and see if he could get the wheezy, ancient environmental systems running again.

Something to do, even if it was futile. Something to keep himself focused, not on what had happened, but on what would.

24

BELTRAIRE HAD STUDIED THE STAR MAPS for the area around Wuhtmu during his trip to that far-flung planet. He'd examined the specs for the planet itself, and double-checked what he knew about the backup base there.

He had forgotten that it specialized in agricultural research. He always forgot that other scientists worked those bases. He only thought of them in terms of stealth tech, which he had to keep secret.

But there was quite a little scientific community in Olita, the small town nearby, and they were making all kinds of breakthroughs on agricultural research for the Empire.

Midway through his trip, he found himself hoping to hell that the scientists had gotten the message about the possible destruction of the base. He'd made sure that was sent, along with actual commands to the computer systems so that the secondary backups would start.

So, he was feeling particularly impatient as he eased the ship out of FTL. He planned his arrival so that he was far from a local base that maintained a stationary orbit around Wuhtmu. The base was not Empire military. It was owned by some local militia, which had built the base hundreds of years ago when the Empire was a perceived threat, not part of their community.

Apparently, the militia members *still* thought of themselves as a separate legal entity. The Empire kept an eye on them, but as long as they remained on their orbiting base and in their little town on the surface—thousands of miles from the backup base near Olita—the Empire didn't bother them.

He wished he could. Whatever their sensors might have picked up would be useful to him.

But he was just one person on a strange mission, and the last thing he needed was to tangle with some radicals with an agenda he didn't understand.

He powered up his systems, letting information flood them, since the systems couldn't handle updates while in FTL. He kept the ship back while he stared at the screen, waiting to hear what happened to the backup bases while he was traveling, when a flaring red light caught his eye.

Flaring red almost never happened on Empire systems. That was for the most extreme emergency. The destruction of the three backup bases so far hadn't merited a flaring red.

He was hesitant to open it, but he did.

The station was gone.

The station he had just left, the research station where he had confronted Quint and warned him about Rosealma, where the primary stealth tech research was being done out in the open, where the best scientists were, doing the best work—it had been blown to bits, not fifteen minutes ago.

The update said that all but three people were accounted for. Everyone else had managed to evacuate successfully.

Three people. The information he got didn't tell him who those three were. Were they the ones behind the explosions? Or trying to stop the explosions?

He sank lower in his pilot's chair and threaded his hands behind his head. This was worse than anything he had expected. How could some-one have destroyed the station?

The backup stations made sense. They were mostly unguarded, and no one—not even the people who entered them daily—had any idea about the other layers of the stations.

But this station was guarded, heavily. He protected it well, and so did Quint, even with his fascination with Rosealma.

Then Beltraire froze.

She had been touching stealth tech jars, moving around the station in a suspicious manner. She knew more about stealth tech than anyone.

Had she set up the station to blow? She would know how to do it in an undetected manner.

Beltraire had memorized all of the evac routes. He was the one who had set them up. He knew who was supposed to get on what ship without having to check.

So he tried to reach Quint first, hands shaking. Those three people who hadn't responded, those three unaccounted for people, they bothered him. He couldn't think of anyone the Empire dared lose. The scientists were doing good and valuable work. Quint was brilliant, as were the rest of the Imperial Intelligence officers on board. The security forces were good, and so was the cooking staff, and maintenance and—

He couldn't reach Quint's ship. There was no response at all. As if the ship did not exist. Because if the ship was traveling somewhere, it should have pinged back to him—even if Beltraire couldn't connect with the person he was trying to reach.

He finally gave up, hoping against all hope that Quint had taken a different vessel. Maybe he had been too far away from his evac area.

The information that Beltraire had gotten hadn't let him know what exactly happened or how much time there'd been between crisis and evacuation.

The fact that all except three made it, though, meant there was enough time to empty the station. And he hadn't been gone that long, so that meant there hadn't been a lot of time.

But enough.

He felt his own race against time. He had come to Wuhtmu to stop the last attack, and he needed to. But he had to try one last thing first, one thing that might help him find out what was going on with Quint.

And with the station.

Beltraire pinged the third-in-command for Imperial Intelligence on the station, Anjali Pope, and, to his surprise, she answered fast.

"Where the hell are you?" she asked. "Your ship didn't evacuate."

She had checked on him then. That made him feel good for a half-second, until he realized that Quint hadn't told her about this mission.

"The backup stations are being destroyed," Beltraire said. "Quint sent me to investigate some problems at a station that's still intact, after the first one blew, but then a second blew, and a third. I'm now near a different backup station—"

"You know about the main research station, right?" Pope asked.

"Not in depth," Beltraire said. "Was it deliberate?"

"Explosives in the stealth tech tubes," she said. "I'd call that deliberate. We couldn't defuse. We had to get out."

And Rosealma had been handling those tubes.

"I can't reach Quint," Beltraire said.

"I haven't reached him either," Pope said, "but I'm not worried. Yet, anyway. I suspect he left with Rosealma Quintana."

That made Beltraire start. "Why would he do that?"

"Because we all suspect her of doing this," Pope said. "And don't tell me you don't either, because you're the one who's been screaming about her from the beginning."

"Oh, I do. But you think Quint is involved?" Beltraire asked.

"I think he's trying to prevent her from getting away," Pope said. "She's using her own ship, instead of her evac vessel. I've been able to verify that much."

"Do you know where she is?" Beltraire asked.

"The ship I'm on doesn't have good tracking capability. I'll be shifting to an official vessel shortly. Then I'll go after her." There was no emotion in Pope's voice. Usually she didn't sound this breathless either. She was clearly shaken, and doing her best to deal with it.

He probably sounded the same way.

"What do you need?" she asked.

"If you can reach someone on Wuhtmu," he said, "maybe send a squadron here or something. This is one of the few sites left, and we have to protect it."

"I'll do what I can," Pope said. "What will you do?"

Good question, he thought, but didn't say.

"Right now, the station's intact," he said. "I'm going down there, to make sure that it doesn't blow."

"Sounds dangerous," she said.

He shrugged, even though he knew she couldn't see him. Yeah, it sounded dangerous. But he had no other ideas, and time was running short.

He wasn't sure what he had been thinking, coming here alone.

"Have you contacted…" he almost said *the secret research station* and stopped himself just in time. This was an open channel.

The station he and Quint manned was well known. Everyone in the Empire knew it did stealth tech research.

But there was one more station, one only Imperial Intelligence and a handful of scientists and engineers who had high-end security clearance knew about. The most dangerous stealth tech research was done there, and the biggest breakthroughs had come from that site.

He couldn't warn them from here.

"There's one more location that we haven't discussed," he said, trying to figure out how to phrase this so she would understand him quickly. "You need to get protection there. And when I get done here, I'll meet you there."

There was a momentary hesitation. Did she fail to understand him? He would need to figure out what to say if she didn't understand this.

"Oh, shit," she said, as the realization hit. "I'll make sure protection arrives immediately."

"And don't forget my backup," he said.

"Second on my list," she said.

As it should be. Second, even though that made things harder for him.

He had no idea if Rosealma knew about that second large research station. She might have, even though it had been built during her years away from the Empire.

He had no idea if she had the clearance to know about it or if Quint had let information about it slip.

And Beltraire didn't have time to figure it out either.

He had his own mission to complete.

Before it was too late.

25

QUINT FELT WOOZY. He still leaned against the door into the cockpit, staring at Rosealma. The screens on the *Dane* were dark, at least from this perspective. But he wasn't entirely certain. Lights flashed across his eyes, and that worried him.

The skin on his face was tight with dried blood. He probably looked terrible—as terrible as he felt. Somehow, somewhere, he'd stopped crossing his arms. Now his right hand braced him against the wall, keeping him upright.

Rose hadn't seemed to notice. He couldn't quite read her expression—anger? Frustration? Pride?

Then she jutted her chin forward and said, "I know for a fact that no one died when that station blew."

Good God. She was feeling defensive. Her tone was almost belligerent. That surprised him, but he tried not to let the surprise show on his face.

"That's why I left last," she was saying. "I made the computer system check for anyone else."

The fury he'd been trying to tamp down threatened to overwhelm him. He made himself take a breath before he spoke, but he wasn't sure that was going to help.

"And if someone else was on that station, what would you have done?"

He managed to sound calmer than he expected, almost emotionless. He would have been proud of himself, only he thought about all the people he knew, hard-working scientists who had fled for their lives, leaving their research behind. Good people who had been doing their best.

Her eyes widened ever so slightly. And he felt the fury grow. She hadn't had a plan at all.

He brought his arms up and crossed them, nearly losing his balance in the process. He pressed his shoulder against the doorframe and hoped that would be enough.

"Tell me, Rosealma," he said. "You only had five minutes left. What would you have done?"

"Something," she said, her voice small. She bit her lower lip. He wasn't even sure she was aware that she had done so.

"Something." He couldn't stop the sarcasm. Maybe he didn't want to stop the sarcasm. She could have killed so many people—and once upon a time, she had gone after him for not having compassion in the wake of great death.

The fucking hypocrite.

"Don't lie to me, Rosealma," he said, no longer trying to hide his fury. "You wouldn't have done anything. You couldn't. There wouldn't have been time. You would have run to your little escape route and hoped for the best."

She flushed, and that flood of color into her still-beautiful face was a confession all by itself.

Then she clenched a fist. He knew that pattern. He braced for it.

He had caught her in a moment of weakness, so she was going to turn it on him. She was going to make it all about him.

"How come you didn't go to your evac ship?" she asked.

And there it was: the change of subject. Another confession, really. Because she couldn't let the conversation go in a direction that made her see what she had done.

She never looked closely enough. Her holier-than-thou attitude always, always left destruction in its wake. And she never took the blame.

She took an unsteady breath, probably to calm herself.

He thought for a moment: should he answer her? Or should he push more on her intentions in those last minutes before the station blew?

The problem with answering her was that it made him vulnerable. He started to shake his head at himself, but stopped because it made him dizzy. What was wrong with vulnerable, now? After all this time.

Beltraire had been after Quint for caring too much about Rosealma, and it was true: he did. Even now.

He wasn't sure if it mattered that she knew how much he cared. He was at her mercy at the moment, anyway. She knew how to fly this damn thing. She had picked the route.

He marveled at himself: It was the easy questions he could never really answer. The emotional ones.

Why had he come here? Truth for her, and for himself.

"I wanted to make sure you got out," he said quietly.

Her mouth turned upward. She didn't believe him. "Don't lie to me, Quint."

Maybe that was why he was never honest with her about how he felt. "I'm not lying," he said. "If you remember, I tried to get you out earlier."

"I do remember," she snapped, "and I told you to leave. You did. But you didn't go to your evac ship and now I want to know why."

Because he knew she would come here. Because he felt responsible for her. For the station. Because he knew she had been behind those explosions, that destruction.

Beltraire would be angry with him, maybe even use this against him.

Quint hated that Beltraire had been right.

Rose seemed to think this silence was some kind of answer to her question—and maybe it was.

That flush on her face had grown deeper.

"What if I hadn't come to this ship?" she asked. "You would have died. This ship is tied to me. You couldn't have gotten it out of the station."

"But you did come," he said. He had known she would. He *knew* her, whether she liked it or not. Not the scientist-her or even the saboteur-her. But Rose, the woman. Her patterns.

He loved her. He always had.

"The ship is registered to you, Rose," he said.

She was staring at him, and in that look, he saw her. The woman. The one who said she would love him forever. The one he *believed* when she said she would love him forever.

"You still use my name," he said.

That openness on her face vanished. It was as if a door had closed.

He had said the wrong thing, gone too far. Or maybe they were too far gone as human beings to have the discussion he had just started.

She pivoted in her pilot's chair, and worked the control panel. So typical. She didn't want the emotional discussion, so she closed him out and worked on something else, thought of something else, almost as if he wasn't here.

He could see some of the coordinates from this angle.

"You changing our course, Rose?" he asked.

"Just making sure it's correct." She lied to him. She had changed course, and he didn't know why.

He was so tired. The banter bothered him. The loss of the station had shaken him. The deaths—Kashion, and maybe others—they were eating at him.

The loss of the research station at Desierto Amarillo. The investigations Beltraire was handling.

These were not small things. Rose was trying to destroy everything he had worked for, and he didn't even know how to talk about that.

He didn't know how to talk about anything.

26

DANYA KOH RAN OUT OF THE MOUNTAINSIDE, heart pounding. She looked around for a trail, but she didn't see one. Noor had told her there would be a trail, one that she could take to the place he had hidden the ship.

She had suggested hiding the ship, back when they landed, knowing that there would be cameras everywhere. She didn't want the ship anywhere near the station, so no one could trace them. No one could catch them.

But she didn't see the trail. Instead, she saw the ship, much closer than she expected. She nearly wept with relief. She wasn't sure how much time they had, which meant the ship was in danger. She was in danger. They had to get off this mountainside before the station blew.

Timing wasn't guaranteed because of all that dust and the malfunctioning equipment and the age of the station itself. She should have been more prepared.

They all should have been more prepared.

But Noor had come to the rescue again. He had the ship close, the entrance open, the ramp down. She ran up that ramp like a crazy woman, no longer caring if she ended up on some camera feed. The feeds would probably be destroyed anyway—if there even were feeds. No one seemed to care about this place.

They probably wouldn't care that it blew.

She staggered inside the ship, and Noor brought up the door behind her. He told her to get in her seat, which she didn't argue with. She strapped herself in, wiped a hand over her dust-covered face, and suddenly the ship screamed upward. Straight up—going vertical to get them as far from the mountain as possible.

Thank everything she believed in that the ship was new, made at Lost Souls as an experiment—a long, narrow ship that looked like it belonged in the Empire but had the most advanced technology.

Because they needed the long sleekness for their escape, and she needed to believe in the tech. Because, in that moment—as they tried to make a maneuver that the ship's engines screamed against—she knew that Noor was more frightened than she was. He had asked her a dozen times what would happen when the levels underneath that mountain blew, and she had told him a dozen times that the mountain would implode, but it seemed like he hadn't believed her.

He had believed something worse would happen.

He got them into orbit so fast that Koh's head spun.

Technically, they shouldn't be orbiting at all. Technically, they should have fled immediately. But they were in sync, she and Noor.

Neither of them wanted to leave until they were certain that they truly had completed their mission.

So he floated a screen between them that monitored the mountain from afar, using their own equipment, not hacking into anything nearby. That had been an option, one both of them had rejected, but now part of Koh regretted it, because she wanted to know if they had been caught on camera—any camera, anywhere.

She supposed it didn't matter. If nothing happened, and she was beginning to be afraid that nothing would, then no one would be looking for them.

But if the mountain blew—

Then it did. Or rather, it started to crumble in on itself. It leaned slightly to one side, as if someone had gotten it drunk, and then it folded inward, like a suit of clothes that for a brief moment had held the shape of their wearer, and then fell to the ground.

Only as the mountain toppled and leaned, as its parts fell inward, the force of the explosion—because that's what it was, a massive continuous explosion—pushed debris outward.

She hadn't expected that—rocks and equipment and dust all flying sideways on all sides of the mountain.

She leaned back, forcing herself to exhale. Because it hadn't mattered—all that prep, keeping the scientists away, getting the others to evacuate.

It hadn't mattered.

The homes and the villages and the entire area around that mountain—for miles and miles and miles—they were all going to be damaged or most likely destroyed.

Because of what she did.

She glanced at Noor. He wasn't monitoring their equipment. He was looking at the images coming from the surface as well.

His dark eyes met hers.

"You saved our lives," she said.

He tilted his head just a little, then offered her a bitter half-smile.

"I figured if someone was going to survive," he said, "it may as well be us."

27

BELTRAIRE WAS JUST ABOUT TO HEAD INTO FTL AGAIN, when the notifications reached him. More emergency messages.

The station on Zargasa was gone. The entire mountain was destroyed. The loss of life in nearby towns and villages would end up numbering in the thousands.

He bowed his head. Maybe if he had gone there, this wouldn't have happened. Maybe if he had arrived and warned the station officials, seen it for himself—

Well, if he had done that, he would be dead too. Because the timing was such that he would have been on the ground and talking to those in charge about the time the mountain imploded.

Another implosion. Another backup station gone. Four backup stations, the main station, all destroyed on this day.

That left Wuhtmu and the secret station.

He had to believe that Pope would take care of the secret station.

He needed to get to Wuhtmu.

He needed to save one of these stations.

He sent another urgent message to Wuhtmu. No one had replied to the previous messages.

He could only hope that the staff there was taking action.

He could only hope that it wasn't already too late.

28

IT FELT LIKE THEY WERE TALKING IN CIRCLES. Vague accusations, and half-hearted admissions. Quint's head ached, and Rosealma watched him from her chair, as if he was someone she didn't even recognize.

He finally confessed, let her know that he had tracked her for years, and he was glad she hadn't confronted him about it. The old Rose would have accused him of stalking her. Maybe he had.

It had been hard to let her go.

And he should have. Because he had brought her to the station, the station was gone now. And who knew what else was going on?

Besides Rose, that is. She knew, even though she lied to him about it. Even though she faked outrage.

How dare you ask me if I'm behind all of this? she had snapped at him. *How dare you?*

Because, he probably should have said, *if you hadn't been behind it, you would have been sobbing in your chair at the loss of life, the loss of research. You forget, Rose. I saw you lose research and lives once before. You didn't act like this.*

But he was too woozy to deal with it. Too tired of the lies.

They had fought the way they always did, in circles, and it always left him tired, angry, and upset. And feeling like he was less than he really was.

He asked, tiredly, "What are we going to do, Rose?"

She sighed, closed her eyes for a brief moment, and shook her head, just a little. Then she opened them, and studied him as if she hadn't really seen him before.

Behind her, the images on the screen seemed unfamiliar, stars he didn't recognize. He hoped it was simply his exhausted brain, unable to put the images together. But he worried that she had taken him somewhere he didn't want to go.

She grabbed medical kit, stood up, and walked over to him. She took his chin in the fingers of her left hand, and tilted his face slightly.

The pressure of her fingers made his entire jawline ache. The tilt made him dizzy.

"I don't know where we're going," she said, deliberately answering a question he hadn't asked. Or maybe she hadn't heard the question properly. Or maybe he hadn't asked it right. Maybe he had asked where they were going, instead of what they were going to do.

His knees felt wobbly. It almost seemed as if she was holding him up with her left hand on his chin.

Then she took her hand away. He wasn't entirely tracking. She had put on gloves and he hadn't noticed. She had cleaning strips wrapped around the fingers of her right hand.

She brought her left hand back up and grabbed his chin again. He'd once heard that pain was clarifying, but it wasn't. It was distracting.

"What happened to you?" she asked.

"Cloris Kashion saw something embedded on one of the stealth tech tubes," he said. "She decided to remove it."

Rose bowed her head so that he couldn't see her eyes. The pressure on his jaw grew.

That embedded something—Rose knew what it was. Probably because she had put it there.

His heart sank. He kept wanting her to be innocent, and he kept seeing evidence of her guilt, even as impaired as he was.

And there was no doubt about it: he was quite impaired.

He told Rose about the explosion—at least, he thought he told Rose about the explosion. And she nodded, eyes still shielded from him.

But that grip on his chin got tighter and tighter, as she grew even more tense.

He could see his own blood on her right fingers. She grabbed more strips, not even bothering to wrap them around her fingers this time.

She just wiped off his face, which hurt like a son of a bitch. Little needles digging into every inch of his skin.

"I can't work like this," she said. "We need to do this right."

Whatever that meant.

"Come with me," she said, and led him into the room he'd been hiding in. She grabbed the bed, pulling it down, and removed the bedding.

He clung to the wall. She moved a table close, and put some kind of surgical instruments on it, along with cleaners and maybe something to put him under.

He shouldn't trust her. Beltraire would tell him not to trust her.

But Quint was feeling tired and queasy and he was going to pass out anyway. He had no idea what had been in that tube, but when he had described how close he had been to the explosion—he had described it, right? He didn't remember the conversation wrong, did he? He didn't imagine it—Rose had winced.

Then she looked worried. And shortly after that, she said she needed to look at his wounds.

"You're too tall," she said. "I need you to sit here." She patted the edge of the bed. "In fact, it would be better if you were on your back. Then you won't jerk in pain and I won't have to worry about hurting you worse."

Had he jerked already? It was a blur. He hated that.

He sat on the edge of the bed, right where she had indicated. Then he leaned back and folded his hands over his chest. If she was going to kill him, he hoped it would be fast.

But he knew her. She wasn't the kind of person who could kill like this. Not anyone. Not one on one.

She was a doctor and once upon a time, she had cared about lives. She still did. She didn't have to evacuate the station, and she had done so.

She looked upset when he told her about Kashion. Rose had retreated into herself, that thing she did when the emotion was too much.

He closed his eyes, then reminded himself to open them. She wouldn't hurt him if she could see his expression, if she could see *him*.

She put some kind of anesthetic on his face. It stung for a moment, then everything faded. He couldn't even feel her fingers on his skin. He could hear the clink of glass into a small bowl, see the shards as she removed them from his face.

He had a lot of that stuff in him, and he had no idea if it poisoned him somehow. Maybe that was why he was woozy, why he couldn't seem to keep track of everything.

She worked methodically, a slight frown between her eyes.

Finally, she said, "You're going to need to see a real surgeon. You'll need a double-check on my work."

She removed her gloves and dropped them into a bin beside the bed.

"Your work is fine," he said, or tried to. He was slurring his words because of whatever she had spread all over his face.

"No, it's not," Rose said. "You'll have terrible scars if you don't see someone soon. I don't have the equipment to properly fix the skin. I'm going to do a scan for somewhere nearby that has good medical facilities. I'll change our course and drop you there."

He didn't want to be dropped, although it would probably be a good move. He sat up, still woozy. Then he raised a hand to touch his face, and see what she had done. He shouldn't touch it. He let the hand drop. He could look in a mirror, if he could just stand up.

"Then what will happen to you?" he asked.

"I'll stay until your surgery is over," she said.

He tried to smile. It hurt, even with the numbing agent.

"No you won't, Rosealma," he said. "You'll leave the minute they take me into the facility, not that it matters. The Empire is looking for you and they will find you."

She went cold. "What do you mean?"

"I mean that before we left, I let the authorities know that you were the one who blew the station. I gave them the identification information for this ship. They'll track you, find you, and put you in prison, Rose."

She looked at him in disbelief. "Why would you do that?"

"You killed Cloris," Quint said. He actually felt calm. It was probably the drugs. They were making him a lot more honest than he usually would have been in this circumstance.

"Not according to imperial law, I didn't," Rose said.

He flinched. Or maybe he didn't. The muscles in his face weren't working. Which was good at that moment, because she had just admitted to murder.

His ex-wife, the woman he still loved.

Murder.

But something had changed in his face because she added, "Besides, there's no proof I did anything wrong."

She wasn't the woman he remembered. That woman would never have offered an excuse for a death, especially one at her own hands.

"There wouldn't have been proof," he said sadly, "if you had gone directly to your evac ship, Rose. But you didn't. You came here."

"You came here too," she said. She was so defensive. She had known it was wrong, and done it anyway. "It would have been easier for you to evacuate. You had already given the authorities my information. There was no reason for you to join me."

No reason. There was every reason. She wouldn't even have been in Empire space if it weren't for him.

But he didn't say that. Instead, he said, "You need me."

Her eyes flashed. Anger. He hadn't expected that.

"Why do I need you?" she asked.

"Because I'm the only person who can prevent you from disappearing into the bowels of the Empire's prison system."

"You sound like I've already been tried and convicted," she said.

"Yeah," he said.

He was going to have to explain it to her. All of it. And maybe, just maybe she would listen. Because he really was her only hope.

29

THE BOAT BARELY MADE IT to the dock on the island thirty miles from the backup site. Or what had been the backup site.

Cleta had had Etheni seal all the windows in this pilot's house, and he was glad as hell he'd grown up around boats, or the two of them would be dead now.

The waves had nearly swamped them a dozen times. Etheni had screamed and held onto her chair. He'd told her to strap in, then contradicted himself, because for a few minutes, he actually thought the boat would capsize.

But it didn't.

He did have to use instruments, though, to get them to the island, because they were riding through a hellscape. The air was black with debris and smoke. The bits of ash that fell on the boat's windshield had charred bits that might have been bone.

He didn't tell Etheni that. She was a scientist and thought she was hardcore. She hadn't lived through two different wars like he had, back when he'd served in a peace-keeping force on Decur, one of the Nine Planets. He'd seen enough terrible things done to the human body to last a dozen lifetimes.

When it became clear that three people were still in the station, he should have pressed the remote. Etheni had a look of wild panic in her eyes ever since she had done so, and it wasn't just because the boat was dipping and rising on waves twice its size.

He knew how to deal with tough decisions. Etheni thought she did, but she didn't, and the decision she had made an hour ago would break her.

He didn't want to be around to see that.

The pilot house didn't have an actual environmental system, like a spaceship, so smoke had seeped in despite the seals. His eyes were burning by the time they reached the dock, and he had to keep wiping at them with the back of his hand.

As they got closer to the dock—or the place where the dock should be—his mouth went dry. He couldn't see it. It showed up on the instruments, or rather, on the map built into the system, but he couldn't see it.

Some of that was the roiling smoke, which seemed to be growing worse, and some of that was the frothing water. But it wasn't frothing against anything.

It was frothing *over* the dock.

He cursed, then looked at the island itself. He could kinda see some trees up head, but he couldn't see any ground.

He'd picked this island because it was the highest, nearest point above sea level. He had figured the explosion would cause serious waves that would swamp some of the low-lying islands, but he hadn't expected those waves here.

He should have.

He glanced over his shoulder at Etheni. She was in her chair again, clutching the arms, her knuckles white, her fingernails red with the pressure her hands were putting on her fingertips. She was chewing her bottom lip and it had started to bleed.

She would be of no help to him.

He leaned farther forward, trying to see the instruments, trying to figure out what he could do.

Their ship was on this island, far enough above the waterline—he had thought—to protect it. From what he could tell, that was probably true, but he couldn't be certain.

He hesitated for a moment: should he disembark, see what he could find? And then he realized that he would be leaving Etheni alone on the boat. If a big wave hit—and one would—she wouldn't know what to do.

If they left here and waited the waves out, he could return and find the ship, see what had happened. Because he couldn't go to another island. They would all be suffering the same fate.

He had only a moment to make the decision. He glanced around the pilot house. The air was gray with smoke. He could at least get away from that.

He made himself blink, focus, and look at what they had brought. Their gear, yes, but none of it included boots or any kind of gear that would get them through the water.

And he had no idea if the water was filled with rip currents or something that would pull them into the Seltaana Sea. That settled it. He had no choice.

He swept the boat away from the island and headed into the open water.

He expected a *What the hell are you doing* from Etheni. She would have asked him that this morning, before she'd pushed the remote. She would have asked him a lot of things.

But she said nothing. He wasn't even sure she noticed.

They would have to ride this out, and he had no idea how long that would take.

Or if they would even survive.

30

SHE DIDN'T UNDERSTAND HIM.

Quint could see it in her face. Rosealma thought he was the enemy. She didn't trust him, and she certainly didn't think he could save her from anything.

He had gotten off the bed, and was now leaning against the wall; he wished he could walk away, wished this stupid ship was bigger, so that he had somewhere private to go.

If he walked away, he didn't have to be honest with her. That was his default. Walking away. He could control his desire to trust this woman.

But he couldn't walk away right now.

Instead, he walked toward her. He was taller than she was, his feet a bit wobbly. She held herself to her full height, but he could see it cost her. She didn't want to look over her shoulder at the controls.

She was actually afraid of him, afraid he would take over her ship.

He probably should.

He shook his head, not sure of himself, which was an odd place for him to be in. He usually was so certain of what to do next.

He said, softly, "When the *Dane* entered imperial space, I was actually hopeful. I thought you had come back to help us."

He wasn't sure why he had told her that. Maybe it was self-defense for him. Maybe he was justifying his decisions, not to her, but to Beltraire and all the others.

"I did come back to help you," she said.

She meant it. She actually meant it. She thought her actions would be *helpful*, instead of the most damaging thing she could do.

"No, you didn't," he snapped. "You didn't come here to help us. You came back to destroy us."

Her cheeks flushed, and her eyes flashed with an anger so sudden, it was visceral.

"I did not come to destroy you," she said. "People who destroy things kill people."

He snorted. She was delusional. How had he missed that before? Rosealma thought that she did one thing when she was actually doing another.

"You killed Cloris," he said.

Her lips thinned. "I got everyone out of that facility. Cloris wasn't following orders."

Rosealma never would have made that argument in the past. She hadn't believed that people should die just because they didn't do what they were told.

"You didn't follow orders either," he said, sweeping his hands sideways. She had gone to the *Dane* after all.

And so had he.

He was beginning to see that as a mistake.

"I didn't come to destroy you," she said again. "I came to help you."

Her insistence on the lie was breathtaking. He wanted to take her by the shoulders and push his face against hers, trying to force the reality of what she had really done into her brain.

But he'd never be able to do that. All he would do was make her angrier.

So he stepped back, so that he wasn't tempted to touch her. Then he clasped his hands behind his back, so he wouldn't gesture or reach out or do anything that she could misinterpret.

"I wanted to believe you were coming to help, Rose," he said. "I wanted to believe that you could stop all of the deaths from stealth tech. You're smarter than anyone else when it comes to this stuff."

She didn't seem to hear that last. She was looking at his arms, his hands. Did she expect him to hurt her? He had never touched her in anger, not once in their entire volatile relationship.

He would try to make her understand one last time.

He said, "Rose, didn't you ever wonder how you got in so easily? Why no one cared that you'd been gone for so many years?"

Her mouth opened a little as she understood that he had brought her to this place, not because he felt he owed her anything or even because he needed to see her (and maybe he had; he didn't have time to look at that right now). He had brought her because he thought she could contribute.

After she had spent all of that time in the Nine Planets, reviving her research, he thought maybe she had the solutions now.

He really had thought the deaths would stop.

He tilted his head back. "I *believed* in you, Rosealma. You're brilliant. I honestly thought you could fix it all."

"I did fix things," she snapped. "Just not the way you wanted."

And that was their problem. He always assumed they had the same opinions about the same things, and they never did.

He sighed ever so softly. "You just set them back some, Rosealma. You didn't fix anything at all."

Her jaw set, and that furious look made him want to tell her that he had discovered she was destroying the backup sites too, but he didn't say it.

He didn't want her to know he was on to her. Because if he did, this conversation would get even more difficult. He might even have to take action he didn't want to take.

He would have to do that anyway. At some point, he would have to take control of this ship and bring Rosealma in to face justice.

But he had one last question, one last thing she needed to clear up for him.

"What happened to you, Rosealma?" he asked. "You used to love this work, Rosealma. You didn't believe in destroying anything."

Her mouth opened, then closed. She shook her head ever so slightly as if she couldn't believe he asked that question.

And that one movement, that one small movement, made him want to take the question back. Because he knew, the moment she had shaken her head, that whatever she was going to say, it would be disingenuous.

She would never answer that question directly.

And it was the most important question of all.

31

THE ROVER LOOKED SMALL against the tall stalks of wheat. The rover's exterior was covered in dust from the path that Bhatt had parked it on. From here, Faber couldn't see the station at all, and she wanted to. But it was hidden behind the wheat, swaying in the breeze.

The breeze wasn't enough to counteract the heat and humidity. Drops of sweat ran down her back and soaked through her shirt.

Bhatt didn't look much better. Sweat outlined his shoulder blades and streaked the dirt on his arms.

The rover chirped at them in greeting—he'd smartly set up the remote access so that the moment the rover recognized them, it would open its doors. One of those doors slid inside its pocket right now.

Bhatt didn't wait. He hopped from the ground into the darkness beyond.

Faber was too small to hop. She had to stop, lift a leg, grab onto the hot side of the rover, and climb in.

The interior was beginning to cool down, but it had that sharp wheat smell that she knew, somehow, she would smell in her dreams.

Bhatt had already found the driver's seat and was climbing in it. The door closed behind Faber, startling her.

"Set it off," he said.

"Can we leave?" she asked, meaning, *will the rover work?*

"Of course we can," he said.

"I don't want to get caught in the explosion," she said.

"Then sit your ass down," he said. "We're leaving now."

She didn't have to be told twice. On a tiny screen in front of her, grainy images of wheat and the roads and some of the hazards beyond— hazards she couldn't really identify.

"Activate the explosions," he said, and he sounded irritated. She shot him a glance. He was frowning at the controls, moving his hands across the buttons and knobs that she didn't entirely understand.

Empire equipment was so damn backwards. It was easily breakable, and it looked so very old.

"Activate—"

"I heard you the first time," she said, wondering who had put him in charge. She certainly hadn't.

But he was right. The explosions needed to start.

All it would take was one. Just a squeeze and everything would disappear.

The rover's engines rattled and shook the entire vehicle. Bhatt opened his mouth as if he was going to give her the instruction yet again.

To shut him up, she extended her hand so they both could see the remote, and then she pushed the center of it with her thumb, much like she had when they had left the station.

Bhatt's tablet, which he had somehow linked to the control panel, flared into life. A tiny little alarm appeared in the corner, confirming that a tiny explosion had occurred in the station.

"How many do you think it will take to ignite the gas?" he asked her.

She had no idea. It depended on how airtight the facility was, and she had never been able to fully determine that. The administrators thought they were safe from exposing any of the nearby civilians to a toxic gas leak just by the location of the facility itself—deep in a field, far from Olita and every other village in the vicinity.

The rover tilted slightly, and the tablet slid on top of the console. She grabbed the tablet with her free hand. With the other hand, she set off a dozen more tiny explosives, using her thumb to activate them every single time.

Bhatt opened the shutter on the windshield in front of them. The wheat still waved, but it was below them. He was making a gigantic U-turn, so that they could get to their actual ship and get off this godforsaken planet, when the entire tablet buzzed.

Faber glanced at its screen, saw two dozen flares and activated alarms. She toggled, so that she could see if the flares translated into actual fires and as she did, she heard *and felt* a whooshing-whomping sound.

Bhatt cursed and grabbed at one of the levers.

"We're not far enough away," he said.

She looked at the telemetry. They were being pulled into the vacuum caused by an influx of air as the gas was igniting.

The resulting overall explosion would be catastrophic.

She reached for the controls, not sure exactly what she was trying to do. Bhatt didn't have time to instruct her. He was struggling, cursing, trying to hold a lever that seemed to vibrate out of his hands.

The rover had turned on its edge, the windshield facing toward the bright blue sky.

The sun looked like glowing wheat, with wispy clouds over it. It was beautiful, something she would never forget—if she survived this.

"Help me," Bhatt said.

"Do what?" she asked, because she really didn't know. She hadn't piloted one of these things, and Empire equipment—

"Something's broken," he said. "The rover's not responding. We're—"

The rover rolled at that moment until it was upside down, a maneuver she had lived through in space a thousand times, but not in real gravity, and not with a vehicle like this.

Items that weren't latched down—everything from the tablets to the remotes to shoes (and they weren't hers) streamed past her face, slamming against the ceiling of the rover.

Then it rolled sideways, and just when she thought Bhatt might have it under control, the roll continued, making her dizzy. The land-sky-wheat-dirt-sky imagery coming through the windshield didn't help. She needed to focus on something.

"We're going to crash." Bhatt said that calmly, as if he were resigned to it.

But she wasn't. She reached for the levers. She was smart. She could figure out equipment on the fly. She would have to—

And then another whomp shook the rover, and debris hit them from all sides. Flame and heat and smoke slammed into the windshield, and the rover turned over and over and over and over and then the windshield broke.

The heat hit her face with such force that she involuntarily inhaled, and knew, as the heat scorched her mouth, her throat, her lungs, that she had made a huge mistake.

32

BELTRAIRE HAD EVERYTHING SET UP on his control panel so that when he emerged from FTL, he would be flooded with information—and he was. Information about the destruction of the main research station. Information about the explosion at Decision Heights. Information on yet another explosion at the Seltaana Sea station.

And then, here on Wuhtmu—images, sent directly to him, from the director of the scientific station of a fire that looked out of control.

Only when Beltraire had his system compare the fire's location to the location of the backup station were his worst fears confirmed.

The station was gone. It had blown up while he was traveling here in FTL. He found the footage of the explosion. The station looked profoundly small and pedestrian inside a large wheat field.

Then white gas seeped out of the doors and windows, spreading slowly, like little clouds. That seemed oddly benign, until a large bang echoed, although he saw nothing different.

Except that the cameras recording the images shook, and the wheat bent toward the building, as if the stalks were being pulled.

Pulled and stripped. Something was sucking them out of the ground, yanking them toward the station, some kind of reaction.

As he had that thought, the entire station exploded, and the nearby cameras went dark.

What he saw after that was something filmed from above. That never-ending acreage of wheat was all aflame now. Burning red and orange and a little blue. Some of the flames licked high into the sky.

He thought he saw some kind of land-to-air vehicle caught in the mix, flipping and out of control, and then it disappeared into the flames.

Whoever was on board was clearly gone now.

He pounded a fist against his thigh, feeling the pain run through his entire nervous system. Backups, gone. The station, gone.

Someone—Rosealma?—had planned this beautifully, with clear coordination.

He had ordered a squadron to join him here, and it hadn't arrived yet. He needed to call them off. He needed an investigation unit.

He needed an entire slew of investigation units, all over the Empire.

Damn her. Damn that Rosealma.

He leaned forward and thought of his choices for just a moment: he could go to Olita and talk to the survivors. Or he could head to the secondary backup sites, the unprotected, unencoded backup sites.

Or he could head to the secret station, the one he hoped to hell Rosealma hadn't found out about.

He was behind on all of this. He should have trusted his instincts, and he hadn't.

He shouldn't have listened to Quint. Quint, who would ultimately pay for this. Beltraire would make sure Quint lost his job over it, at the very least.

Beltraire ran a hand over his face, trying to calm himself.

He needed to make the non-obvious choice. The obvious choice was to go to the secret research station. But he had already sent Pope, and reminded her to make sure the work there was protected.

He needed to get to the secondary sites. The unprotected ones. And he needed to figure out how to protect the information that was already there.

He felt wrung out and alone. And determined.

More than determined, really. He was going to catch Rosealma and her co-conspirators.

And he was going to make them pay.

33

GAGNE HADN'T EXPECTED the rendezvous site to look abandoned. Even though she had known it was abandoned—that was why Squishy had chosen it.

The star base didn't just look abandoned, it looked nearly unsalvageable. It was dark and looming, tilted away from her. Larger than she expected, but vulnerable too, with wires and pieces hanging off its center.

No one had repaired it after a ship had plowed through the middle of it, and someone should have. There had been a thriving community here once, and a single tragedy had destroyed it.

She smiled thinly. She had just caused a single tragedy of her own on Telaan. She and Skopf had gotten away only because no one had expected the destruction of the mountain. They were dealing with all the dead and debris and the avalanches and the storm and everything she and Skopf had left behind.

No one had followed them. No one had probably even realized what the two of them had done.

They probably wouldn't realize who had done this for days, maybe even a week.

By then, any trail she and Skopf had left would be cold.

They weren't supposed to be at the rendezvous point long. Squishy had said leave after twenty-four hours, no matter what happened. If no one else arrived, leave. Even if everyone arrived, leave.

They had to head in their separate directions.

Gagne wasn't quite sure why the rendezvous was even supposed to happen. A victory lap, maybe?

Although it didn't feel like a victory to her. The adrenaline she had felt after the fight through the ice storm, then the massive explosion, and then the escape, had dissipated into an odd feeling of malaise.

If she hadn't felt that malaise in the past after a major adrenaline rush, she wouldn't have known what she was feeling and what caused it.

She turned slightly in her seat, and looked at Skopf. The medical equipment they had on this ship had patched him up, but he still looked odd. His face wasn't red anymore, but the white patches remained on the tip of his nose and on his cheekbones.

He glanced at her, and awkwardly touched his right cheek. She had no idea if those white patches hurt, but he was clearly conscious of them.

She ran a scan of the station, not expecting much. Surely whoever arrived would have gotten it going—turned on some lights somehow, done something.

Which meant that they were the first.

Skopf tapped the screen before them. "Look at that," he said, sounding relieved. "Someone else is here."

Gagne looked at the information before her. A single life sign, not two. And a ship she didn't recognize.

Mentally she cursed Squishy. They hadn't prepared well for this part at all. They should have known what kinds of ships the other teams had. They should have known who was coming from where, and what had happened.

They should have known a lot of things.

But Squishy had been scared that they would get captured and reveal what they knew.

Gagne's hands hovered over the controls. One person, not two. That was bad enough. She had no idea if the person waiting here was part of a team, and if they were, why another team member hadn't come with them.

She didn't command ships or run actual teams. She didn't make decisions like this for a living. She wasn't really a leader.

But Skopf seemed to be waiting for her. He frowned at her.

"What's the problem?" he asked.

"How do we know if that's who we're supposed to meet?" she asked.

He looked at the heat signature, then at the make of the ship, and then he shrugged. "Does it matter? There's one of them. Two of us."

"That's the problem," she said. "There's one of them."

His gaze narrowed as if he was trying to understand what she was saying. Then he sighed.

"There was nearly one of us," he said.

She looked at him sharply. He had a point. She smiled just a little at herself. The adrenaline was gone, and in its place were all the emotions she had suppressed earlier in the day.

Including fear.

"Right," she said. "Of course."

Then she paused.

"And if that person is here to…" She didn't even know what word to use. Arrest them? Fight them? None of that made sense. If the Empire had figured out what they had done, and had figured out where the rendezvous point was, then they would have had a large presence here, not one person.

Skopf was still staring at her. She shook her head.

"Never mind," she said. "I'm being silly."

He nodded, which irritated her. He shouldn't have nodded. He shouldn't have agreed with that.

She gripped the edge of the console before her, let the pointed metal edges press into her palm, felt just a little bit of pain.

She made herself focus. She needed to take those emotions that were springing up inside her and tamp them down. This mission wasn't over yet.

They had to get through the rendezvous, and then, somehow, get home.

She and Skopf hadn't even discussed how they were going to do that. They would, maybe after the rendezvous.

"All right," she said. "Let's dock."

This day wasn't over yet. Not even close.

She had to move forward, even though she didn't really want to.

34

For decades, Rosealma had been trying to talk with Quint. The stealth tech deaths had clearly haunted her, and he hadn't listened to her about them.

When he lured her back to the Empire, he had thought she would work with him to prevent more deaths. And when she dug in and worked hard at the research station, he had wanted to tell Beltraire that he was wrong about Rosealma, that her desire to prevent more deaths was going to get her to improve stealth tech, make it something they could all use.

The woman standing across from Quint, her expression defiant, wasn't interested in improving stealth tech. She wanted to destroy it, make it not exist, make it disappear forever.

He leaned against the door frame on the *Dane*. He still felt odd, as if his brain was wrapped in gauze. He probably shouldn't be having this conversation. He should take her into custody, and fly this thing to the nearest space station.

She was watching him closely, as if she was trying to figure him out.

And then her forehead furrowed.

"Oh, dear," she said, sounding concerned. "You're bleeding again."

He raised a hand toward his face.

"Don't touch it," she said.

Rosealma came toward him. She put her hands on his shoulders.

"I don't know what got in those wounds," she said. "But something's keeping them from healing. I don't want you to spread it."

Spread it how? he wanted to ask, but didn't. She moved him ever so slightly, so that he was backing into the second room.

She slapped a hand on the wall, and the bed came down with a bounce.

"Sit there," she said, all business. Like any other doctor he'd had. Never a request, always a command.

He hated the commands. They made him feel like something had gone really, really wrong.

Now he wanted to touch his face or maybe even grab some kind of mirror and see what the damage really was.

She grabbed the medical kit, brought it over, opened it, and selected a numbing agent.

Her fingers hovered near his left eye. It ached just beneath the lower lid. Her fingers were uncomfortably close.

"Close your eyes for just a minute," she said.

He did. She wiped the numbing agent along his cheeks. It ached where she touched him, and then turned cool. He knew from experience that the coolness would fade.

Then he felt a small prick in his neck just above his collarbone.

"Hey!" he opened his eyes. She was tossing an anesthetic vial back into the kit.

He tried to sit up. There would be something to counteract the anesthetic in that kit. He would have to find it before he passed out.

He reached for the kit, fingers tapping, as he tried to pull it toward him.

But she pressed him back against the bed, and the damn anesthetic was working because he couldn't grab the end of it. He couldn't push her away. His muscles weren't working like he wanted them to.

"Hey," he said—or hoped he said—or thought he said.

He wanted to add, *Rose, don't do this. Rose, we can figure out how to mitigate the damage from everything you did. Rose, we can try to find a solution that works for all of us.*

144

But the words never came out of his mouth. They swirled around in his head, and he couldn't force them out, wasn't sure if he should force them out, really, because she had destroyed an entire research station, cost at least one life, maybe more, and maybe she was behind that other destruction, maybe she had done more...

The thoughts spiraled away. He was drowning in darkness. He reached for her, but probably didn't move at all. He was reaching, reaching, reaching—

And then he passed out.

35

THE WAVES FINALLY SUBSIDED. The air was still a grayish brown. The smoke would hover over this area for hours, maybe days. It was giving Cleta a headache. Or maybe that was all the stress he had just endured, from fighting with the boat to keep it upright, struggling to make sure that he and Etheni would survive long enough to make it back to their spaceship.

If the damn ship had survived the gigantic waves.

The explosion had been so large that it had destroyed much of the island that held the station. That was why there was such a large reaction. He hadn't expected it, and Etheni certainly hadn't. They had thought that only the station would blow, but she had done something wrong, or overcompensated, or underestimated what other kind of research was inside that building.

His muscles ached from trying to keep his balance while fighting with the controls. Etheni actually looked green, something he'd rarely seen on anyone. She'd lost her stomach contents twice as the boat rose on the swells, and then she'd moaned as if each movement made her dizzy.

She was of no use to him right now.

He felt time passing with every single second. The nearby authorities, whoever they were, would search for the culprits.

Cleta couldn't count on the authorities thinking that the culprits had died in the explosion. Although he and Etheni nearly had—or rather, nearly had died in the explosion's aftermath.

He scanned his equipment to see if the Seltaana Sea had calmed. It looked like it had, from all of the readings. Unlike a storm, these waves were caused by a single event, something that was a one-and-done. Once the force moved through the water, nothing would follow.

And so far, nothing had.

He turned the boat around. Now he had to see the damage. He needed to know if the spaceship got damaged when the second island flooded.

He would need Etheni to help him once they arrived, but he didn't tell her that now.

Let her wallow in her seasickness. He reached inside the small cooler underneath the front of the boat and removed a sickness tonic. He handed the bottle to her.

"Drink," he said. "You'll feel better."

He had no idea if he was lying or not. He didn't care if he was. The drink would settle her stomach and replace some of the fluids she lost. She might not feel better, but she would at least be able to help him.

And that was what he needed right now.

Just a little help, and they could escape.

36

THERE WERE THREE SECONDARY BACKUP STATIONS, stretched across the Empire. All of them were in well-made ancient buildings near strange and equally old underground sites. The sites were historic and predated the Empire itself.

But they were all so well built that the buildings and the constructions had been used throughout the Empire's history, often for covert and important purposes.

Beltraire wasn't the person who had designated the sites for the secondary backups. He had inherited them—or rather, Quint had. But Beltraire was the one who was trying to get them decommissioned.

He had wanted six new backup sites, located across the Empire, and he had been lobbying for that long before this crisis occurred.

His stomach ached, and he kept swallowing bile. He felt off-balance, unable to calm himself, which was rare for him. Events were moving too quickly; he wasn't sure how to take command of them, which was something he apparently needed.

He had just landed on the flat landing area in the middle of a series of hills. The landing area used to be part of a mechanism from below, something that looked like the hilltop, but the weight of time and the hill itself eventually broke the system.

No matter how hard Empire technicians tried to fix that mechanism, they couldn't. The technology was both unfamiliar and unfathomable to them, like other bits of ancient technology scattered through the Empire.

So, sometime before Beltraire learned about this place, someone sheared off the fake hilltop and paved it over, making a semi-secret landing area.

He always found landing here tricky when he was piloting himself. The hills were close together, and flying between them at low altitude required a skill set he had but rarely used.

Landing here this time made his stress levels rise—and they were already high.

He suited up—something he'd learned the hard way at one of these sites years ago, when he had arrived and the environmental system had failed. He didn't want to enter an area where the air was bad without a suit ever again. But he kept his hood down. He wouldn't use it unless he needed it.

His environmental suit was tight, but it looked formal, just in case he encountered any workers. It had the Enterran Empire seal over his left breast, and the black material made him look formidable.

He needed that since he was alone. Sometimes the people left at sites like this were protective of their tiny fiefdoms. He didn't want to wrangle with any one of them, especially since he was here alone. He wanted to make sure that they knew who was boss.

He disembarked onto a windy plain. The air smelled of pine and dirt, smells he had forgotten even existed until this moment. The wind poked at his face, swirled his hair, and made him feel like a thousand little bugs were marching across his skin.

He hated natural environments. They made him feel vulnerable, which was something else he hated.

He loped to the small door that was built at an angle against what remained of the original hilltop. The door was gray and striped with reddish brown water marks. It took him a moment to realize those weren't water marks, but rust stains.

He stiffened. Nothing should be rusted here. But no one had contacted him either, not when everything started to go bad.

He opened the panel over the door controls, and activated them. The door struggled to open for a moment, banging against its frame as if it were rusted shut.

Then it squealed open. He stared into the darkness for a moment, not liking what he saw. The last thing he wanted was to get trapped inside this thing.

He looked around for a rock, found one the size of his head, and used it to prop the door open. The door still rattled in the wind, so for good measure, he grabbed two more rocks and put one next to the first rock, and the second where the door latched, just in case the door somehow managed to break free of the first two rocks.

With that done, he slipped inside.

No lights came on as he crossed the threshold, not even emergency lighting. The air smelled stale and old.

He'd been in a number of places like this throughout his career, and he knew that when the lights went, the environmental system was gone as well.

That didn't mean the secondary backup had failed. There was no reason for a continual presence at this site. There wasn't really a need for any guards either, as long as there was off-site monitoring.

He turned on the lights on the front side of his suit, so that he could see what was ahead of him. The air was filled with dust and debris. The environmental system was definitely off.

He grabbed his hood with his left hand and pulled the hood up, setting the seal before turning on the suit's internal environment. If he remembered this site correctly, the backup network was one level down. If the main level was this compromised, the lower level was probably worse.

No alarms came on as he walked; no one notified him. It had been nearly a decade since someone from Imperial Intelligence had visited this place. He had no idea who was in charge of maintaining it, if anyone.

He had been warning Quint for a long time that the secondary off-site backups weren't secure, but Quint hadn't listened. He had thought the entire system was protected.

Besides, Quint once said, who would want to steal stealth tech? It was all stored so deep in the Empire that no one would be able to access it.

He apparently hadn't expected that someone would want to destroy the technology altogether. Or that he would know the person who wanted to destroy it.

Beltraire shook his head. The air in his suit was cooler than the air outside. He could feel the difference in his nostrils. And he was more comfortable. He hadn't realized how uncomfortable he had been until the suit had found its equilibrium.

The corridor led to stairs. He remembered this place now. There was no elevator between levels—the elevators had been deemed too danger-ous. He would have thought that they would have been replaced as well.

But this place looked and felt abandoned. A shiver ran through him. He hadn't monitored any of this. He wasn't even sure who was in official command.

He had simply inspected it for its use as a secondary backup, figuring no one would want to come here. In the original design, the information backed up here was information that was older. The regular backups, the daily ones, were done at the sites that had exploded.

His mouth suddenly went dry. He had a moment of worry: what if someone was trying to destroy this place? What if they did try to destroy it while he was here?

Then he shrugged. If they did, they did. But he was seeing no evi-dence of interest, no way that someone had been here recently enough to set explosives.

The only way this place could be destroyed was from orbit, the way that the Desierto Amarillo site had been destroyed.

And he had scanned for ships in orbit before he arrived.

He had seen nothing.

He let out a tense breath. Then he went down the stairs. They were some kind of metal and rang as his boots hit them. That sound seemed abnormally loud, which made him realize that this building was abnormally quiet.

He reached the bottom of the stairs, and lights came on. A cooling system activated, and red lights appeared around a large door, warning him to go no farther.

He actually smiled. The upstairs had been a decoy for an unguarded station. It was letting anyone who arrived here know that there was no value in this place at all. Nothing to see here, nothing to steal.

If they ventured down to this level, though, they would discover the truth of what they were seeing. There was something of value here, and it was dangerous.

He opened the door control panel and used his personal code to unlock the door. For a moment, he thought the code wasn't going to work. And then it did. The lights changed to a pale yellow, which apparently was normal, and the door clicked before sliding back into its pocket.

He stepped inside. The door remained open, which relieved him, since he didn't have rocks to brace it with. Ahead of him were rows and rows of gleaming equipment, all of it appearing pristine and humming with activity.

He walked closer, glancing once over his shoulder at the door. It remained open. He hadn't commanded it to close, so it didn't.

He walked deeper inside, remembering to turn off his suit lights. The equipment was clearly functioning. He went into one of the center modules, built in a slight U-shape, and entered his own passcode, then looked to see if the information had been updated in the last twenty-four hours.

The site had received dozens of backups in the past few hours, after receiving none for the past week.

He let out a breath, feeling just a little relief. But he kept looking, making sure the site had received information from the guarded backup sites, as he had ordered, not just from some random location.

And it had. Information had come from three of the sites that were destroyed in the past hour.

His request had gotten through.

Now he needed to get guards on this site, and make sure nothing happened here. He would have to figure out how to do so, before this place got destroyed.

He would also send someone else to check the other secondary sites. Then he would secure the information.

He paused, running his hand on the edge of the equipment before him. He could feel the ridges through his glove.

He would do one other thing. He wouldn't tell Quint that this secondary backup site survived.

Beltraire found it shocking that he believed he couldn't trust Quint. But Beltraire had come to that during this long, confusing day. Even if Quint was on the right side—the side of the Empire—his trust in Rosealma had nearly destroyed all the work everyone had done.

Beltraire couldn't allow that to continue.

When this was all over, he would talk to the Chief of Imperial Intelligence and let her know everything that Quint had done.

Quint could no longer remain in charge, that much was certain.

And Beltraire had an idea—a good one—as to who should replace him.

37

TWO OTHER SHIPS WERE DOCKED on a tiny bay on the side of the space station at the far end of the Empire. Koh looked at the floating screen, which showed the only part of the station that had life.

The rest of it looked like the relic from a war fought long ago. Walls were gone. Ropy pieces of something, maybe something vital to the station's environmental system, hung off what must have been floors or ceilings or sides of the station.

It was impossible to tell now which side the space station had once considered "up," back when it had full gravity and a lot of ships docking at its many bays, probably on the way from here to somewhere else.

Now this was the ass-end of the Empire, such a backwater that anyone on the teams who knew the Empire well thought this would be a safe place to gather.

Only two ships bothered her, though. It bothered her as Noor approached the station, bothered her as he found a place on the bay and started to fly in, bothered her enough to make her say, *Let's not dock too close to the others.*

He glanced at her then, his dark gaze unfathomable. She had thought both of them were in sync not a few hours before, but now it felt like he had receded into himself.

They had watched the damage on Zargasa as long as they could, the entire mountain spreading out as it went flat, the power of the avalanches knocking everything in their paths, destroying a place she had lived in for months of her life.

Probably destroying people she had known for those same months.

She was trying not to think about that. She was doing this because she believed stealth tech was evil, that it would destroy millions of people over time.

Only she had just added the word *millions* today. Because before, she used to say *thousands*. And she, just today, might have destroyed thousands all by herself.

She still hadn't washed her face. She wasn't sure she was ever going to wash her face. She was going to wear the dirt from that mountain, that base, like the shameful badge it was, at least through this rendezvous.

Noor, to his credit, hadn't told her to clean up either.

He had docked the ship, but didn't shut it down entirely. "We're not staying here very long," he said, and she nodded.

She didn't want to be here long, no matter what Squishy had ordered.

Koh and Noor hadn't discussed where their next destination was, and she was glad for that. Because she didn't want either of them blurting it to those who had already arrived here.

As far as she knew, this was a head count. Squishy wanted to know who survived and who hadn't. Koh and Noor would stay long enough to be counted, but after what happened today, Koh didn't really care how many of her compatriots survived.

They had all done their bit, and now it was time to move on with their lives.

The bay doors had closed shortly after the ship arrived, and a notification had been sent to their controls, letting them know when the environment had been reestablished.

Koh hadn't expected environment here at all, so that was a pleasant surprise. Still, she and Noor wore their environmental suits, expecting the environmental controls to break down at some point. Neither of them wore their hoods. Their suits were sealed around the neck, wrists and inside their boots, but there was full gravity here as well, which was also a surprise.

155

Noor led the way off the ship. Koh followed down the ramp, waited with her back to him as he closed the ship up. She heard the metallic door snap closed behind her, and she almost turned around and rushed back to it.

But she didn't.

This part of the station had a working environmental system. Someone had turned it on recently, though, because the air smelled stale and old, the odor probably coming from the ducts and the station itself.

The lights were grimy and gray, but there was no debris in this bay, nothing that suggested the damage that she had seen when they arrived. The air was cold. The environmental system hadn't been on long; it still needed time to get to optimum temperature.

She wouldn't be here for that.

When Noor reached her side, they walked up toward the only open door. Noor glanced over his shoulder once, as if he was checking on the ship, checking to make sure the bay doors were still closed.

She didn't bother to look. The environmental system would be behaving differently if the doors had suddenly opened.

Her boots clanged as she hurried toward that open door. She wanted to leave already, and the only way to do that was to get this out of the way.

The door was bigger than it looked. It opened on a wide corridor that had probably once been busy with incoming passengers. Now, it was just the two of them.

Another door stood open to their right, and with a start, she recognized the layout. This was the way to customs and registration, but if the travelers wanted a meal and a drink first, the arrival bar was on the right.

She had been in half a dozen Empire space stations decades ago with the same layout. And, in all of them, she had been one of the people who had scurried past the restaurant/bar so that she could find a place to relax and unwind, without the stress of arrivals continuing onward.

She walked through the second open door, surprised that the lights were brighter here. It was also warmer.

Three people sat at an actual U-shaped bar, the stools bolted down. There was no other furniture here, no alcohol, no smells of beer or wine or some kind of fried food. That same stale stench covered everything, reminding her that this place was damaged and beyond repair.

She recognized the faces of the three sitting there, but not where they had come from. The moon-faced man was István Gorka. She hadn't liked him when they'd gone on their last retreat, and he gave an even stranger vibe now.

She stayed away from him, looking instead at the other two. Dagmar Gagne sat closest to the door, her face lined, her environmental suit bunching in the middle as if it was too big.

Next to her sat Clay Skopf. His skin was mottled and his eyes were a little too bright. He nodded at them as they came in.

"Success?" he asked.

"Of a type," Noor said. They had already agreed not to talk about how catastrophic the explosion had been. "You?"

Skopf smiled thinly. "Of a type as well."

"How come there are only three of you?" Koh couldn't remember who had partnered with whom.

Squishy had asked them all to forget as many details as possible and Koh had done that except—apparently—everyone's names.

"Hallie didn't make it," Gorka said. Something in his voice made Koh stiffen. He clearly wasn't grieving, but there was an emotion in his tone, an emotion she didn't recognize.

She probably should have empathized with him, losing his partner and all, but something in that tone made her even warier than she had been before.

Noor seemed to feel it too, because he stiffened beside her. "Shouldn't everyone be here by now?" he asked.

"It takes time to get here," Gagne said, as if they hadn't made the trip themselves.

"I got here first, hours ahead of them." Gorka inclined his head toward them. "Managed to get some systems turned on, which surprised me."

"We helped," Skopf said, and in that single sentence, Koh thought she heard *we did most of the work.*

She didn't want to be here, now more than ever. "No sign of Squishy?"

"No," Gagne said.

"Or any of the others?" Koh asked.

"We're supposed to be here twenty-four hours," Gorka said. "I'll be here more than that."

"Why exactly are we supposed to be here?" Gagne asked, shifting in her seat so she could see him.

"Head count," Noor said.

"And confirmation that the work is done," Gorka said. "If not, I'm sure Squishy will send some of us to finish the job."

"If she gets here," Noor said. Then he looked directly at Gorka. "After all, your partner didn't make it, and Squishy was working alone."

What Noor didn't say was that she was working on the hardest part. The actual research station. Koh didn't feel like saying that either.

"What do we do if she doesn't arrive?" Gagne asked.

"Follow orders." Gorka sounded strangled, as if those words hurt. "We leave."

"I don't like being here now," Koh said. "I really don't want to wait."

"I don't blame you." Skopf's voice was soft. "But I think it's prudent to find out what happened."

"I don't." Noor sounded almost angry. "This just makes it easier for the Empire to round us all up and take us all in. Someone wasn't thinking clearly."

He didn't say Squishy, but they all knew that was who he meant. Maybe none of them were thinking clearly. Koh hadn't been. She should have considered what would happen when the mountain collapsed.

But she hadn't been raised in gravity or on land, and living near that station was the longest she had ever been landbound. There were things she hadn't considered about what she had done because she hadn't done enough study of something she didn't think she needed to study—the way things actually worked on land.

How mountains collapsed—if, indeed, they ever did.

Her eyes filled with tears, and she wanted to wipe at them, but to do so would call attention to them.

So instead, she crossed her arms. "I'm not waiting," she said, knowing she sounded like a petulant child. "We completed our mission. We're not going on another one. We're done."

Gagne stared at her. Skopf half-smiled, as if he understood the sentiment.

Gorka nodded. "Look," he said, "I'm staying. I need to be in one place for a little while. So I can tell Squishy or whoever shows that you've been here and were successful. If you're okay with that?"

"I prefer that," Koh said. She glanced at Noor, to see if he had any objections. She had doubted he would, and she was right.

"Thank you," Noor said, and executed a tiny bow. Then he took Koh's arm as if he were the one in charge, and pulled her toward him.

She didn't object. They were a team, and he wanted out as much as she did. She didn't want to make awkward conversation. She didn't want to wait for the Empire to arrive.

But most importantly, she didn't want to see Squishy ever again.

Koh let Noor turn her around. They walked out the door and back the way they came.

Now the dirt on her face felt heavy. It itched, and she wanted to wipe at it.

She would clean it off when she got inside their ship. When they were heading far away from here.

She would wash all of it from her. And then she and Noor could decide where they were heading.

Together.

38

BEEPING WOKE QUINT UP. His eyes felt glued shut, and his face ached, particularly his cheeks. His mouth tasted like old socks dipped in something bitter, something chemical.

His back was pressed against a wall, and his hands clutched something soft, like carpet.

His eyes fluttered open. The space he was in was oval-shaped, padded, and small. Through a door carved in the padding, he could see another room, and an actual control panel. There were portals, showing the blue-blackness of space, stars winking in the distance. Nothing else.

He wiped at his eyes. They were dry too. The air was slightly cold here, and he shivered. Across from him was a floor-to-ceiling cabinet marked *kitchen* and *supplies* in Standard.

With that, then, he knew where he was. He was on an escape pod.

Rosealma had drugged him and gotten him to the pod somehow, and then launched it far from the *Dane*.

Dammit. He should have seen that coming.

He opened the cabinet, saw that a section folded down to create a tiny kitchen, one that would allow him to cook and keep food cool. There were plastic dishes and utensils, wrapped and attached to the wall. He found a container of water, with a capped straw. He removed the cap and sucked greedily, not knowing if the water tasted like chemicals because of the container or because of the lingering (awful) taste in his mouth.

The beeping was going to drive him crazy. It hadn't gotten louder, or even more rapid, but as he slowly came to himself, the beeping had become more obnoxious.

He set the water container back in its holder, remembering to replace the cap only at the last minute. Then he braced a hand against the padded wall. This damn pod was designed for people who had no idea how to pilot anything. He hoped it had proper controls.

He tried to stand, discovered his legs wouldn't hold him without wobbling, which he figured was the effect of the drug still. So he crawled into the main area and pulled himself up on the control panel using his elbows and arms, hands turned toward himself so he wouldn't accidentally push any controls.

His legs still wobbled while he was on his knees. He found the control that made a chair rise out of the floor, then he climbed into the seat. The movement left him short of breath.

Damn Rosealma. When he found her, he would…oh, he had no idea what he would do. Because he had no idea where he was, or where she was. Or how far he was from anything.

He had let the Empire know about her ship. He had also let them know about the tracers he had planted months ago. The Empire was searching for her, and they would find her, but he had no idea if she would tell them about him, drifting out here.

He couldn't believe that she hated him enough to let him die here.

Although, if she wanted him to die, she would have killed him on her ship and shoved him out the airlock. And she could have done it leaving no trace. Just an overdose of something in that medical kit of hers.

Or she didn't even have to overdose him. She could have knocked him out, like she had done before putting him here, and then shoved him out of the airlock. He would have died in space and no one would have been the wiser.

She hadn't tried to kill him.

There was that, at least.

The beeping wasn't the emergency beacon which—to his surprise—was on. The beeping came from the tiny communications array. He had to flick a switch to turn it on.

"…if you can respond, please do so. We have your location, but we are twelve hours out."

The voice was an actual human voice, not an automated one he had been expecting.

He scanned the tiny array for a way to respond. And then he found it. Another toggle, also clearly labeled. He had expected this to be harder.

"This is Edward Quintana. I'm all right, but I've been injured, and I'm weak. I will need medical assistance when you arrive."

"We will bring medical assistance," the voice said. "Are you able to hold on for twelve hours?"

"Yes," he said. "I'm in an escape pod, and it seems undamaged. There are supplies. You have my location?"

"It was sent to us, encoded, and then we picked up your emergency beacon. We've been trying to hail you for several hours."

Several hours. Rosealma was gone then. Long gone. But his location would help them find her location.

They would get her, and then he would oversee her punishment. He needed the Empire to take it slowly, because he didn't want them to damage that mind of hers.

If she wasn't willing to help them with stealth tech voluntarily, she would help them involuntarily.

He would see to that.

"My location was sent to you," he said, suddenly realizing that Rosealma might have tricked him again. "You're with…"

"Lacuna Star Base," the voice said. "We serve the Enterran Empire from here. You don't need to worry, sir. You're still in the Empire."

He felt his shoulders relax. Rosealma hadn't sent him to one of the Empire's enemies or somewhere that he didn't know.

She had dumped him off her ship, but she had contacted the authorities—the Enterran Empire authorities—letting them know where he was immediately. She had given him medical attention, activated the emergency beacon, and made sure that someone would find him quickly enough to take some kind of care of him.

She wasn't trying to kill him at all.

She was just trying to escape him.

And she wouldn't be able to do that.

She had gotten the better of him on the research station. Beltraire had been right: she had been untrustworthy in the extreme.

But Quint knew that now. He also knew that he wasn't immune to her, no matter how much he had thought he was.

So when they found her—and they would, once he was back with the Empire—he would make sure she paid for this. He would also make sure that he listened to whomever was backing him up. Or maybe he would just deliver her to someone who could manage her.

At least she didn't know about the secret research station, the one where the most important research was being done. She had probed several times about where all the research was being done.

He had told her—truthfully—that it was no longer done at universities because of the accident near Vallevu that had killed so many. He said the best research was being done on the station she destroyed, which was true, and she had asked about the backup stations, which she had known about from her days with stealth tech years ago.

But she had never learned about the unsecured secondary sites, the ones that he had planned to close, and was now relieved he hadn't.

And he could never bring himself to tell her about that secret research station. He had thought, daydreamed maybe, that once she understood what he was doing and she had come back to the Empire completely, he would take her there and show it to her.

He might still take her there.

As a prisoner. To work for the Empire again.

But he would decide that later.

Right now, he needed to rest. Right now, he needed to get better.

Right now, he needed to plot his revenge.

39

THE DOCK WAS DESTROYED. That was the first thing Cleta noticed as he pulled the boat closer to the island. The dock was destroyed and dozens of trees had fallen into the water. He thought he would have to circle the island to find a place to land, but miraculously, he found a stretch of beach that looked like it had been cleared off just for him.

Etheni had managed to down some liquid and hold it in place. Her skin had gone from green to grayish, but she wasn't moaning any longer.

Cleta wasn't talking with her. He couldn't decide if he was mad at her for underestimating the power of the explosives she set. He asked her about it just once, and she muttered something about land and gravity, which sounded like excuses to him.

He didn't need excuses.

He pulled the boat as close to the shore as he could get, then tossed over the anchor. He probably didn't need the anchor because he'd heard the bottom of the boat scraping against the sand. But he didn't really want to pull the boat onto the beach.

He wanted to run for that spaceship, and worry about the boat later. If the boat drifted into the sea, the anchor would hold it into a place where he could swim toward it. He wasn't relishing that, especially given how much his lungs hurt, but he could do it.

The air hadn't cleared. It was still a mass of stinky black smoke and ash. His eyes watered, and his throat burned. Maybe some of the sickness that Etheni was experiencing came from this air, and not from some kind of seasickness.

Or maybe it came from self-loathing.

He had no idea, and again, he didn't care. Once they got out of here, once they got to the rendezvous point, he would ask someone else to take her back to Lost Souls. He was going elsewhere. Where, he had no idea. But he was done being an activist, done being a man of action, done doing things that were marginally ethical.

The anchor caught, and he powered the boat down. Then he extended the ramp to the beach.

Etheni watched him, her hands clasped in front of her.

"You first," he said.

She glanced at him, her eyes glazed. He didn't want to push her off the boat, and he didn't want to carry her. He was going to have to get her moving, and that irritated the hell out of him.

Just as he reached for her shoulders, she jerked forward, as if her body didn't respond properly to her commands. Then she managed to walk down the ramp to the beach.

She stopped at the edge of the ramp and looked at the trees beyond. He wished she'd move slightly to one side, but she didn't. He hurried down the ramp and pressed the button to make it retract, which it did quickly, locking in place with a snap.

He put his arm around her waist and pulled her forward. "Come on," he said.

"Such destruction," she said, but let herself be moved.

Yeah, it was a lot of destruction. Trees down, leaves everywhere, ropy branches covering the beach itself, the sand wet, and water dripping off everything.

Even with the stench of the smoke, the air here also smelled of fish and saltwater.

Something that looked vaguely like a path remained. He didn't remember the path to the ship being a wide one, but his sense of perspective was skewed now that everything had been moved.

He propelled Etheni forward, heading toward their ship, which wasn't that far from this beach. It was just uphill, the grade barely what his legs could handle after all the stress of the day.

As they got deeper in the trees, Etheni seemed to come alive. She shook him off and bent at the waist, using her hands to help her move forward.

It looked awkward, but it worked. She had moved out ahead of him. He followed, noting just how eerily quiet this place was. Water dripped, the ocean lapped, but he couldn't hear birds or insects or the rustling of other creatures, like he had heard when he landed the ship here.

Maybe everything had died.

Etheni reached the top of the rise faster than he did. As her feet disappeared from his view, she gasped.

He didn't like that sound. It probably meant the ship was destroyed. Although it might mean the ship was intact.

Etheni wasn't that verbal at the moment.

But he was bracing himself, as he climbed the last few meters, for the ship to be completely destroyed. Then he would need another plan.

He crested the rise and saw the ship, gleaming blackly in the weird gray light filtering through the smoke cloud. The ship wasn't damaged. It wasn't even wet. Everything on the rise was intact. The water hadn't made it this high.

He looked for Etheni, but didn't see her. She was nowhere around. Maybe she had gone inside.

He wouldn't put it past her.

He rounded the front of the ship, heading toward the entrance that led to the cockpit, when a dozen soldiers, all dressed in black, surrounded him. They wore the Enterran Empire insignia on their left shoulders, and they were all holding laser rifles.

Those rifles were trained on him.

He held up his hands, marveling that his breathing remained even, his heart rate unchanged. He had been in bad situations before. He'd learned from them, learned that if he handled himself correctly, he would be fine.

Besides, it was hard to be upset about an arrest after just surviving a bombing and a tidal wave.

He scanned the soldiers, looking for Etheni. She was being held between two more soldiers. When she saw Cleta, she burst into tears.

"I'm sorry," she said—and it seemed like she was saying that to him. "I should've planned better. I should've realized what the explosions would do. I should have—"

"Just shut up," he snapped, glad he was an entire row of soldiers away from her. Otherwise he would shove her down the hillside or maybe grab her too hard by the throat or something.

The loathing he hadn't realized he felt for her rose like a live thing.

They were here because of her. They could have escaped if she had done her job as she promised she would do it.

Destroy the station, not the island. Escape to the boat. Take the boat to this island, and not have to dodge tidal waves. Go to the rendezvous. Go home.

It had all sounded so simple, and of course it wasn't.

Cleta had no idea how the Empire treated prisoners like him. People who attacked science and research stations like him.

But he knew one thing: he could say he had no idea what she was going to do. She had set everything. He had merely handled the getaway.

"Who's in charge?" he asked, ignoring Etheni.

A man Cleta hadn't even seen peeled himself away from the side of the spaceship. He looked expectantly at Cleta.

"I am," the man said. "What of it?"

"I'll talk to you," Cleta said. "No one else."

The man eyed him as if he'd never heard anything like that before. Etheni was bleating Cleta's name. Cleta ignored her. He knew that whoever talked first—or maybe, whoever talked—just might survive this entire encounter.

"All right," the man said, turning his back on Etheni. "Let's hear what you have to say."

40

BELTRAIRE MADE IT BACK TO HIS SHIP to find one more piece of good news. Authorities at the Seltaana Sea had picked up the saboteurs. And one of them was going to talk.

The man claimed he had names, locations, plans, everything. The man implicated Rosealma almost immediately.

Beltraire sank into his seat and closed his eyes for a half second.

This had been a hellish day. There would be a lot of loss, a lot of recrimination. Lives had disappeared. Property had been destroyed.

But the research survived. He would make sure that the research from the secret station was properly backed up as well. And then he would put redundancies upon redundancies in place.

It wasn't enough to have secret facilities. They were only as good as the people keeping secrets. What the Empire needed was remote backup facilities with superb security. The Empire couldn't just rely on location to keep those facilities safe.

Of course, Quint would say that they had been safe. They hadn't become unsafe until someone targeted them.

But if stealth tech developed the way that Beltraire believed it should, someone would always be targeting it. Not someone like Rosealma Quintana who knew about stealth tech and had a personal reason for trying to destroy it.

But someone who was an active enemy of the state, someone who was a true saboteur, working for another government.

Beltraire had no idea who that would be—not yet. There might not be anyone like that for decades.

But he would protect against it. And he would guard the information.

He wished he could see Rosealma Quintana now. He would pull her aside and let her talk about her pet subject, how stealth tech was improperly understood, how it was dangerous and how it would harm people.

Then he would remind her that *she* had harmed people, that she had cost hundreds of lives. He would tell her the one thing he believed. The one thing that he now knew to be true.

It took work. It took planning. Sometimes, it took a few miracles.

But the one thing she never understood, the one thing he had relied on from the beginning of this hellish day to the very end, was that knowledge was very hard to kill.

All that work she had done had been for nothing.

And he would dedicate his life to making sure she—or someone like her—could never do anything like that again.

I value honest feedback, and would love to hear your opinion in a review, if you're so inclined, on your favorite book retailer's site.

Be the first to know!

Just sign up for the Kristine Kathryn Rusch newsletter, and keep up with the latest news, releases and so much more—even the occasional giveaway.

To sign up, go to kristinekathrynrusch.com.

But wait! There's more. Sign up for the WMG Publishing newsletter, too, and get the latest news and releases from all of the WMG authors and lines, including Kristine Grayson, Kris Nelscott, Dean Wesley Smith, *Pulphouse Fiction Magazine, Smith's Monthly,* and so much more.

Just go to wmgpublishing.com and click on Newsletter.

ABOUT THE AUTHOR

New York Times bestselling author Kristine Kathryn Rusch writes in almost every genre. Generally, she uses her real name (Rusch) for most of her writing. Under that name, she publishes bestselling science fiction and fantasy, award-winning mysteries, acclaimed mainstream fiction, controversial nonfiction, and the occasional romance. Her novels have made bestseller lists around the world and her short fiction has appeared in eighteen best of the year collections. She has won more than twenty-five awards for her fiction, including the Hugo, *Le Prix Imaginales*, the *Asimov's* Readers Choice award, and the *Ellery Queen Mystery Magazine* Readers Choice Award.

To keep up with everything she does, go to kriswrites.com and sign up for her newsletter. To track her many pen names and series, see their individual websites (krisnelscott.com, kristinegrayson.com, retrievalartist.com, divingintothewreck.com, fictionriver.com, pulphousemagazine.com).

The Diving Universe
(Reading Order)

Printed in the USA
CPSIA information can be obtained
at www.ICGtesting.com
LVHW040338220923
758915LV00001B/32

9 781561 463596